## 'So that's all I was to you—just a brood mare?'

'Not even that, it seems. You don't want my child.'

Not true. Oh, *not* true! She wanted Liam's baby so badly that it was like a permanent ache in her heart. But she didn't dare admit it. Not to him; not even to herself. If she so much as let the thought into her mind she was terrified that he would see the truth in her eyes.

**Kate Walker** was born in Nottinghamshire, but as she grew up in Yorkshire she has always felt that her roots are there. She met her husband at university and originally worked as a children's librarian, but after the birth of her son she returned to her old childhood love of writing. When she's not working she divides her time between her family, their three cats, and her interests of embroidery, antiques, film and theatre, and, of course, reading.

You can visit Kate's website at www.kate-walker.com or e-mail her at kate@kate-walker.com

**Recent titles by the same author:**

THE HOSTAGE BRIDE
DESERT AFFAIR
THE DUKE'S SECRET WIFE
  (*Society Weddings* 2-in-1 short story)
THE SICILIAN'S WIFE

# THE CHRISTMAS BABY'S GIFT

BY
**KATE WALKER**

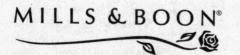

**MILLS & BOON**®

All the characters in this book have no existence outside the imagination of the author, and have no relation whatsoever to anyone bearing the same name or names. They are not even distantly inspired by any individual known or unknown to the author, and all the incidents are pure invention.

First published in Great Britain 2002
Harlequin Mills & Boon Limited,
Eton House, 18-24 Paradise Road, Richmond, Surrey TW9 1SR

© Kate Walker 2002

ISBN 0 263 82989 8

Set in Times Roman 10½ on 11½ pt.
01-1202-51303

Printed and bound in Spain
by Litografía Rosés, S.A., Barcelona

# CHAPTER ONE

*MARRY in haste; repent at leisure.*

Peta turned her head up to the pulse of the shower and let the hot water pour down over her face until the heated pounding numbed her skin. And all the time she wished, deeply and fervently, that she could also make it numb her thoughts.

But nothing would erase the uncomfortable phrase from her mind.

*Marry in haste; repent…*

'No!'

The word escaped her on a cry of desperation and rejection and she hastily reached up and snapped off the shower, closing her eyes against the unwanted feelings.

In the sudden silence, the sound of her uneven, ragged breathing was unnaturally loud and disturbing. The sound of a harried animal, hunted and trapped, cornered with its back against the wall—and knowing there was no way out.

'No…' she said again, more softly this time, shaking her head so that drops of water spun off from the long, deep brown strands and spattered against the elegantly tiled walls of the shower cubicle. 'Oh, no…'

The silence was too much for her. Too heavy. Too disturbing. She had to turn the shower back on to escape the thoughts that plagued her.

'Peta?'

The sound of another voice—male, deep, and resonant, only just avoiding being drowned under the fresh rush of water—came to her from the direction of the doorway

5

between the bathroom and the adjoining bedroom, making her lids fly open, blue eyes staring at the cubicle door in shock.

Blurred and distorted through the thickly frosted glass, she could just make out the shape of her husband's tall, powerful figure, the rich colour of his hair. But she didn't need to see him clearly. Her memory and her imagination could instantly supply every detail of the rest.

And that imagination swiftly sketched in the strongly carved, harshly stunning features: powerful cheekbones, a long, straight nose and darkly lashed brilliant green eyes. The vibrant, glossy gleam of his hair, closely cropped against an unruly tendency to wave, the deep brown shot through with lights of fiery copper that made it burn and glisten in the sun. And all of that set on the tautly muscled body of a natural athlete with wide straight shoulders, broad chest, narrow hips and long powerful legs. Legs that always seemed to be planted so firmly on the ground, as if he was staking his claim to the earth on which he stood, marking it out as his.

'You in here?'

'Who else would you expect to find in your shower—your bathroom?'

Her voice didn't have quite the strength or the genuine lift of humour that she aimed for, but she was struggling with too many other feelings to be able to control it properly. Even at a distance of several metres, just knowing that Liam was there, in the doorway, made her naked skin tingle all over. It was as if the low, faintly husky rasp of his voice was like a caress over her exposed flesh, bringing the blood springing to the surface, and setting a pulse throbbing at her temples.

'Our.'

'What?'

Peta pulled her head from under the running water to listen more clearly.

'What did you say?'

'I said, *our*. Not my shower, but *ours*. Our bathroom too.'

The reproof was low, light, good-humoured, but all the same it sent a shiver running down Peta's spine, chilling her blood in spite of the warmth of the water.

*Our* bathroom. *Our* shower.

Did he know what it did to her to hear those words on his tongue? To catch the deep, dark, faintly possessive note in the sensual voice? To recognise just what it was that had put it there?

To know that what he really thought he possessed was *her?*

To the rest of the world Liam Farrell might be her husband, the man with whom she was supposed to be celebrating her first wedding anniversary this late December evening. But Peta knew that the real truth was very much more complicated than that. And that was what had set her mind on its restless, disturbed pattern of thought for some days now.

'Shall I join you in there?'

'No!'

There had been nothing in the least bit dangerous or threatening in the question. As a matter of fact, it had been asked in the easiest, most laid-back way. But all the same it had Peta stiffening in instant rejection, her heart lurching into pounding in double-quick time.

'Don't!'

It was his silence that gave away his change of mood. The sudden total stillness of the blurred figure seen through the steamed-up glass of the shower door that revealed far more than anything he might have said just how much he disliked her response.

'I—I mean I was just coming out.'

It was simply the *idea* of him doing as he had said that had sent her thoughts into overdrive, her body into the sort of tension that made her nerves scream in protest, her skin colouring in a rush of blood that had nothing to do the warmth of the shower. But at the same moment the image in her head made her pulses race, her heart pounding in heavy excitement. Under the fall of the water, her already heated flesh tingled in sensual anticipation of the pleasure that had become such a dangerous part of her life.

'Okay. Come on, then.'

She could see through the frosted glass that he was reaching for the huge, thick white towel, shaking out its folds, holding it ready. And she knew that she had no excuse not to do as he said. To keep him waiting any longer.

'Peta…'

Was she hearing right? Had there really been a note of warning in the low, steady use of her name? The noise of the still running water made it difficult to decide if it had truly been so or if it was simply her already over-sensitive mood that had made her believe it was there.

'*Peta…*'

No mistaking that voice! The ominous undertone had her rushing to switch off the water once again, smoothing back the sodden dark strands of her hair.

How could she face him, feeling the way she was right now? There was only one way to do it, she told herself. Play it his way. The way it had been from the start of this marriage. The way she knew that Liam wanted it to be, because he had declared that openly to her face when he had not so much proposed as outlined a business venture to her. But for the past few months she had known that she couldn't go along with the original terms of their arrangement, and she had tried desperately to find a way of telling him so.

*Marry in haste; repent at leisure.* Once more the phrase echoed inside her head as she opened the door of the shower cubicle. But she pushed it away with all the strength she could muster, desperately dragging up the smile that she knew he would expect from her and praying it would hide the truth.

*Marry in haste; repent at leisure.*

The words had been plaguing Liam's thoughts all day long. He had woken up with them running on a loop through his mind and he hadn't been able to switch them off for more than a moment since.

He supposed it was inevitable that today, the first anniversary of his ill-considered rush into matrimony, would bring such thoughts to the surface. But, if the truth was told, he hadn't expected the feeling of self-reproach, the kick of *What the hell have I done?* to be quite so savage.

That wedding, just four days before the previous Christmas, had seemed like the answer to so many prayers—so many problems. But uncharacteristically he hadn't thought things through. There had been many developments along the way that he had just not anticipated. And this latest change in his circumstances was one that had knocked him completely off balance. How had he ever got himself into this situation?

'Peta, damn you, are you coming out of there or do I have to come in and—?'

The words evaporated on his tongue, choked off hastily as the shower-cubicle door was pushed open and his wife stepped out.

Damn, damn, *damn* it! Did he really need to ask himself how or why he had trapped himself in this marriage? If he did, then just to look at her gave him his answer.

Silently he cursed his body's instant response to Peta's

physical appearance. He only had to see her to want her—and want her with a force and a hunger that came close to actual physical agony. The swift, brutal tightening below his belt, the twist of desire, was so sharp, so savage he had to bite back a cry of pain, of protest.

'Or you'll come in and…what?'

Did she know just how provocative she looked, standing there, trails of water still running down her stunning body, the normally pale ivory of her skin flushed pink by the warmth of the shower? Did she know what it did to him to see her lush form exposed so blatantly, revealing the high, full breasts, narrow ribcage and waist, the long, smooth lines of hips and thighs, sweeping down to the delicate ankles and feet?

Of course she did! She couldn't be unaware of it. She saw and felt the results of her impact on him in bed every night. It was what had brought them together in the first place. What had pushed them into this ill-considered marriage in such a rush.

Sex, pure and simple. Though there was nothing remotely *pure* about his thoughts right at this moment.

'Liam?'

His silence had disturbed her. Her sapphire eyes were narrowed in confusion, a frown drawing her fine, dark brows together.

Deliberately he switched on a grin that was wickedly provocative, letting his own green gaze sweep over her from the deep brown hair clamped tight around the fine bones of her skull by the water, down to where her small pink toes curled on the soft bronze carpeting.

'Do you have to ask? You know what would have happened… If I'd joined you in that shower you wouldn't have been able to get out. Instead we would still be in there, having wild, passionate sex.'

It was only what she had expected him to say, after all.

Only what he had always said, all through the three hundred and sixty-five days of their married life. If he had said anything different now, then it would have rocked the boat desperately, shaking the foundations they had built this relationship on. And that would be dangerous. It would risk her coming to suspect that things had changed. That they were no longer how they seemed.

And that was something he wasn't prepared to admit to himself yet, let alone to her.

'We still could.'

Invitation sparked in her eyes, lighting their blue depths, and an enticing smile curled the rich fullness of her mouth.

'If you want...'

He was tempted. God help him, but he was tempted when she looked at him like that, with that wicked sparkle in her glance, that curve to her mouth. He could even see just the very tip of her pink tongue where it rested on the edge of her lip. She looked like nothing so much as some small, contented cat that was watching a saucer of cream being poured, anticipating its rich taste with delight.

She was totally unembarrassed by her nudity. Standing tall and proud and straight, completely unfazed by the fact that she wore nothing at all while he was still fully dressed in the elegant silver-grey suit, darker grey shirt and silk tie that he had worn for a business meeting that day.

But then she had to know that she was beautiful. Surely no woman could see her own face as it was now—with its high, slanting cheekbones, the richly coloured full mouth, the deep, deep blue of her eyes—in all the purity of its essential beauty, every trace of make-up and any other artifice washed away, and not know how stunning she was in masculine eyes. In anyone's eyes.

'But you'll have to get rid of the posh suit. You wouldn't want to ruin it...'

The provocation was too much. His heart lurched, his blood heating, a stinging tightness below his belt telling him instantly how much at the mercy of her seductive teasing he was. He had never been able to resist. Couldn't do so now.

For the space of another couple of heartbeats he almost followed her lead. The habits of the past year almost reached out and entangled him in their grip again, unthinking response driving him in an automatic direction before he had time to reconsider. He had even tugged at his tie, loosening it at the knot, smiling into the darkness of her eyes all the time, when reality caught up with him sharply, kicking him hard in the ribs, and made him rethink.

'Perhaps not…'

He tried to make it sound relaxed, casual, indifferent even, and wasn't at all sure whether he'd come anywhere close. Then he saw the change in her expression, the shadows that had clouded the clear blue, and knew that he had succeeded better than he had ever anticipated. Better than he had ever wanted.

But it was too late to back out now.

'Here…'

He held out the white towel, forcing himself to ease the revealingly tight grip on the soft material.

'Better wrap yourself up.'

Reproach flashed from those beautiful eyes, a reproach he fully expected her to put into words. If there was one thing he had learned about this wife of his, over the past year, it was that she didn't mince matters. If she felt angry, or disappointed, or dissatisfied, she said so. But to his surprise she bit her lip visibly, and a faint shiver shook her slender form.

'You're cold.'

He was grateful for the extra impetus to get her to

move. A single drop of water had escaped from the darkness of her hair at her shoulders and was trailing a slow, delicate path over the creamy surface of her skin, and down... It slipped across the curve of one lush breast, touched the rose-tinted tip and hung for a composure-shattering second from the tight bud of her nipple.

Once more hot desire gave him a harsh, burning kick in the gut. Liam swallowed hard, spoke hastily, hunger making his voice rougher than he had anticipated. 'Come on, Peta—don't just stand there! Wrap yourself in this towel and get dry.'

Perhaps he'd been mistaken. Seeing reluctance where there was none. Now she moved forward, into the enveloping folds of the towel, without hesitation, without protest.

The towel enfolded her slim form easily. So easily that it twisted something deep inside Liam. That slenderness was part of the problem. Part of what was fretting away at the fabric of the marriage they had built up together. Peta wasn't still supposed to be as slim as on the day he had married her. Kids had been a major part of their agreement—and one year later there was no sign at all of any baby on the way.

'Thank you—I'm fine now.'

Peta forced herself to say it. She had to say something to fill the uncomfortable silence that had descended. Something to distract him from his awkward question. How could anyone be *cold* in the superbly heated, luxurious bathroom of Liam Farrell's home?

But of course it hadn't been cold that had made her shiver so revealingly. Instead it had been the disturbed state of her thoughts.

'I'd better go and dry my hair or I'll never be ready in time.'

The ease with which he let her go only added to her

confusion and mental discomfort. She had been prepared for an argument, some sort of protest at least. This wasn't the Liam she knew so well. This Liam was in a very different mood from the one she'd assumed he was in from the moment he'd first made that provocative remark about the shower, pushing her to reply in similar vein.

She'd expected that he would try to kiss her, to hold her close. To assert once more the powerful sexual attraction that always flared between them. The same attraction that had had her whole body throbbing in response simply to the sound of his voice. And she had been prepared to handle that.

But not this strange, almost cold indifference.

Something was very wrong here. Something that she had been aware of for days, like the throbbing ache of a tooth that needed filling and wouldn't stop nagging.

Dear God, please let it not be that he had guessed the way she was feeling.

'What's wrong?'

The question came so unexpectedly from behind that she actually jumped like a startled cat as she padded her way, bare-footed, across the rich bronze carpet towards her dressing gown.

'Wrong? What do you mean, wrong?'

Her voice was uneven and rough, revealing her inner turmoil, and the hand that reached out to grasp her hairbrush was not perfectly steady.

'How could anything be wrong?'

'I don't know. You tell me.'

Unhelpful as well as enigmatic.

'Liam, I'm fine.'

His response was an inarticulate sound of sceptical disbelief that had her clamping her fingers too tightly round the brush handle, the skin showing white at the knuckles.

'All right!'

Impetuously she swung round to face him, then immediately wished she hadn't as she met the full force of those brilliant, stunning green eyes head-on.

'All right,' she tried again, less forcefully this time as a new wave of tension gripped her. 'Seeing as you obviously don't believe me—why don't *you* say what's wrong? Why don't you explain what made you ask that question in the first place?'

His shrug was a masterpiece of controlled indifference, one that seemed to shake off her question as totally unimportant. But the casual nonchalance of the gesture was belied by the laser-like intensity of his gaze, the burning focus of those deep eyes on her face. Peta shifted uncomfortably under its scrutiny, feeling as if a much-needed protective layer had been scraped away from her skin, leaving her disturbingly raw and vulnerable.

'I would have thought that today of all days you'd be feeling happy and relaxed. That you'd be looking forward to the party tonight with excitement and anticipation. Instead I find that you're nervy and distant…'

*She* was distant? What about the way he had been the past few weeks? What had made him so difficult, so unapproachable, just at the moment when she had most needed to try and talk to him?

The question almost escaped Peta but she bit it back just in time.

'And if I am distant as you say—have you ever considered that it might just be the party tonight that's making me feel that way?'

Another rough sound of disbelief escaped him and he actually shook his proud head in dismissal of her comment.

'Oh, come on, darling! You know that isn't true—I know it can't be true.'

'And why not?'

'You know why.'

'Tell me.'

Liam moved away from the doorway at last, strolling across the room to stand beside her, looking down into her wary blue eyes.

'I've never seen you nervous—or even unsettled before any sort of social event. Nothing fazes you. And especially not tonight.'

'No.' Peta shook her head, sending her drying dark hair flying around her face.

'No?'

That sceptical note was back in his voice.

'No, nothing fazes you—or no, nothing's wrong?'

'No—not "especially not tonight",' Peta quoted back at him. 'I don't see why you think I should be so easy in my mind about tonight.'

'And why the hell not?'

It was clear that his grip on his temper was wearing thin. The relaxed, drawling voice was becoming rather ragged at the edges.

'There can't be anything to worry you about tonight.'

'Oh, can't there?'

'No—it's a happy event. You know everyone who's going to be here—family and friends. They're all coming to help us celebrate—'

'And that's just it!' Peta broke in, unable to hold the words back any more.

The double meaning of that 'happy event' was more than she could bear. She knew what 'happy event' Liam had been anticipating by this stage in their marriage. She was supposed to be pregnant by now. It was what they had both wanted at the start. What she still wanted, but not in the way she had originally thought.

'What's just it?' Liam frowned impatient confusion. 'Peta, you're not making any sense.'

'Maybe that's because none of this makes sense.'

Peta began dragging the brush through her long dark hair, the rough, abrupt movements mirroring the edginess of her thoughts. The bristles caught in a couple of tangled knots but she didn't pause, wincing faintly as she tugged them down.

'What the—?'

Reaching out, he caught hold of her hand, stilling the nervy gesture with a grip so strong that she could do nothing but submit to his control.

But she didn't have to look at him. She couldn't look at him for fear of what she might read in his face. And so she kept her own head stubbornly averted, staring fixedly down at the carpet as if fascinated by the sight of his polished black leather handmade boots planted firmly on the thick carpet.

Staking his claim again. The memory of her own thoughts earlier came unwillingly to her mind, dousing the fire of her mutiny like a bucket of cold water tossed over a leaping flame.

'Peta, sweetheart, are you going to explain just what is going on inside that delightful head of yours? What is it that is bugging you—and why?'

That 'sweetheart' was just too much. He used it casually, easily, without even thinking. He didn't mean it. Not really. It was just a word, one he dropped into conversation without a care. It was what people—outsiders—expected a husband to say to his wife.

But not this husband. Not to this wife.

And she knew he never thought about the effect it might have. That he never for one moment considered how she might feel, hearing him direct that apparently loving term at her and knowing that it had no place anywhere inside their marriage.

Because love had no part at all in this relationship between herself and Liam.

At least, it had had none at the very beginning. The arrangement was a marriage of convenience from start to finish. No emotions involved in any way. Or, rather, that was how it was supposed to have been. How it had always been on Liam's side. And on hers at first—at the very beginning.

But not now. Now things had changed. Changed so fundamentally that she was no longer convinced that she could continue with this marriage in the way they had decided just over a year ago. She didn't think she could continue with it in any way at all. Not unless things changed in a way that just didn't seem possible.

She had told herself that she would do as Liam wanted. Play it his way. But it was getting so much harder with every day that passed. Because she hadn't stuck to the guidelines, the rules they had so carefully laid out from the moment they had agreed to this marriage of convenience. Instead, she had committed the worst sin of all.

She had fallen head over heels, totally, recklessly, blindly—impossibly—irretrievably in love with this husband of convenience of hers. And that love was the last thing he wanted from her.

And the knowledge of that fact had driven her to desperate measures. For the last few months, she had been actively taking steps to make sure she didn't conceive the baby that she knew Liam wanted, even though it had almost broken her heart to do so.

# CHAPTER TWO

'DON'T call me sweetheart! I don't like it!'

It was the nearest she dared come to expressing the whirling thoughts in her head, the pain that was burning in her heart.

'First I've heard of it—but—fine!'

The nonchalance of his answer made matters even worse, heaping coals on the fires of misery she was already struggling with.

'Is that what's bugging you?'

His expression made it plain that he thought she was really way over the top if she was making such a fuss about a simple word.

'What? No, of course not.'

'Then would you mind explaining just what is?'

The way the words were cut off, sharp, cold and clipped, left her in no doubt at all that whatever control he had had over his temper was now rapidly wearing thin. All it would take was one more hesitation, an attempt to dodge the issue, and he would lose it completely. And Liam in a temper was something she didn't want to risk, especially not tonight.

'It's—it's this party—' she tried again.

'What about the party?'

'I'm not sure it's—it's right.'

'Right?'

The word was clearly the last one he had expected to hear.

'Right?' he repeated, frowning his confusion. 'Precisely what is *wrong* with it.'

'Nothing's wrong with the party. It's just that I'm not sure that it's right for us to be celebrating like this. No—listen…' she put in hastily when he drew a swift, sharp breath in through his teeth, obviously priming himself for some sort of cutting retort. 'It's the first anniversary of our wedding day.'

'A fact that I am only too well aware of.'

The black irony of his tone made her wince but she forced herself to ignore it so that she had the nerve to continue.

'But it wasn't exactly the sort of wedding day most people have. The sort they'd want to celebrate. Ours isn't that type of marriage. It never was and it never will be.'

But she had dreamed that it could be, and that was the problem. She had dreamed of love and happy ever after and those dreams had been stronger even than her longing to become a mother. But it was only as the mother of his children that Liam had wanted her.

'And yet we've invited all these people. My family—your grandfather—friends…'

'They wanted to come. Besides, it's Christmas, and everyone loves a party at Christmas.'

Liam was being deliberately awkward. Surely by now he knew exactly what she meant. She didn't have to spell it out.

But it seemed that she did.

'They wanted to come to help us celebrate. But they don't know the truth of it. They don't know that our marriage is really little more than a business arrangement and not the love match they believe it to be. I don't feel that we have the right to expect them to celebrate something that is little more than a lie.'

'A lie!'

She'd caught him on the raw there, somehow. And it was clear he didn't like it. The stunning features darkened swiftly and with a rough movement he twisted the hair-brush from her hands, tossing it aside, careless of the way it fell to the floor with a soft thud and spun away across the carpet.

The next moment hard fingers closed over her arms and she was wrenched up close to him. So close that she was forced to tilt her chin sharply in order to look up into his face. It was either that or bury her head in his shoulder, and with every one of her senses instantly on red alert at simply being near him she didn't dare to risk any close contact. Already the warm, clean scent of his skin was coiling round her, unbearably provocative, instantly arousing. And his beautiful, sensual mouth was almost exactly at eye level; the temptation to lift her head just a little higher and press her lips to his was almost irresistible.

She could kiss him out of this mood, she knew. At least, she'd always been able to do that in the past. But now, after that awkward moment in the bathroom when he'd completely blanked her, she didn't think she dared to risk it. The thought of another rejection was frankly more than she could bear.

And besides her conscience was troubling her badly, as it had been for months now. When she had mentioned a lie, what she had really meant was her own recent behaviour, the guilty truth she was holding back.

'A lie,' Liam repeated, more quietly, but no less harshly. 'This marriage is no lie, *sweetheart*. It's exactly what we wanted. It's exactly what we've made it—and that makes it a lot more honest than most.'

'But...' Peta tried to break in, nerving herself to tell him, but he swept on, totally ignoring her attempted interjection.

'Believe me, there are many of those who start out believing that their love is for ever who don't even last to their first anniversary. Plenty of marriage vows break at the first hurdle. They fall out of love as swiftly as they fell into it. One crisis and it's over—done. They hate each other and never want to see the other person's face ever again. So...'

Somewhere along the line he'd made a dangerous mistake, Liam told himself; the swift rush of his thoughts faltering, making him lose his train of argument. He should never have come so close. Never have caught hold of her like this. Never have crushed her up against him until they were almost melded into one, thigh to thigh, hip to hip, the softness of her breasts pressed against his chest. The clean, fresh scent of her skin, tantalisingly combined with the delicately perfumed shower gel she had been using, coiled around him, teasing his senses, making his head swim with desire.

His whole body was on fire. So hot that he could only be grateful for the fact that the double thickness of the towel that wrapped her acted as insulation between her skin and the burn of it. That, and the achingly swollen demand of his hunger for her that pressed urgently against the cradle of her hips.

Swallowing hard to ease the raw dryness of his throat, he tried again.

'So—what we have is well worth celebrating.'

'But...'

'But nothing! What we have is what's right for *us!* And that's all that matters in a marriage. That the two people involved in it are getting what they want from it. That it makes them happy...'

A sudden, nastily uncomfortable twist of his conscience almost brought him up sharp, but he forced the uneasiness down again and hurried on, praying she hadn't sensed his hesitation. There wasn't a problem. These things took time.

'We're celebrating a year together—no matter what the circumstances. That's the truth.'

A sudden movement of her shoulders distracted him, drawing his eyes irresistibly to the rounded smoothness of her naked skin, still faintly flushed from the warmth of the shower. Instantly his thoughts were distracted from the argument he was trying to express, diverted on to other, more sensual, more inviting paths.

'The truth is...' Peta began, but he wasn't listening to her.

That shoulder was too tempting. The skin on it was so soft, so delicate. He couldn't resist lifting a hand to touch it, to stroke the gentlest of caresses over its curve, feeling the muscles beneath flex faintly, the shiver of response she was unable to hold back.

'The truth, darling?'

It was a blend of husky sensuality and shaken laughter. He still hadn't got a grip on the way this woman made him feel. The incredible immediacy of his response to her, the instant, burning heat of arousal he felt as soon as he touched her.

'Oh, lady—*this* is the truth...'

Lowering his head, he pressed his lips to edge of her shoulder, where the smooth length of her arm began, and heard Peta's involuntary murmur of delight.

'This...and this...'

His mouth trailed slowly, deliberately, towards the fine, arching line of her throat, stilling over the spot at the base of her neck where a heated pulse raced unevenly. With his face concealed against her skin, he let his mouth curve into a smile of sensual triumph as he sensed her instant response, the sudden change in the rhythm of her blood underneath his soft caress. With careful control he nipped gently at her flesh, eliciting another sigh of abandonment.

'This is the truth between us, darling. The only truth we need.'

His hands were on her skin too, now, fingers drifting over its satin warmth, reminding themselves of the familiar lines of her bones, the dips and curves of her shape. One tangled in the still-damp fall of her hair, tugging lightly, while the other followed a dancing path along the front of the towel, finding the bunched-up spot where she'd knotted it firmly across her breasts and lingering provocatively.

'The truth…'

Peta's echoing of his words was part agreement, part groan of surrender, and against her neck his smile widened. Just the tip of his tongue snaked out and traced an erotic pattern from under her ear to the point where her heated blood raged in a frantic pulse. Then he kissed his way back up again, this time letting his mouth drift round, over the fine plane of her cheek and down, to capture her lips. Her instant response, the way her mouth softened, opening immediately under his, allowing the intimate invasion of his tongue, gave him the encouragement he was seeking.

'The only truth,' he muttered thickly, letting his fingers tiptoe back along the top of the towel, the tiny stiffening of her slender body betraying her unspoken disappointment. 'Our truth…'

This time he trailed his hand slowly, ever more slowly, towards its chosen target. Each movement of his fingertips described a graceful arc, then a full circle, coming close— closer—then drifting away again. Peta's mouth didn't leave his for a second, her kiss was still as strong, as deeply intimate as before, but he knew from the tension of every muscle, the watchful tightness of her whole body, that every ounce of her concentration was centred on just one thing. She was as aware of his touch on her skin as he was, waiting—and wanting—him to achieve his aim.

And when he once again reached the spot where that knot held place—loosening rapidly now under the pressure of the tiny wriggles and twists of response that Peta was unable to hold back, he simply let his hand stay still. Simply let it rest with the heat of one wide, hard palm covering the exposed upper slope of her breast, one long finger tucked just inside the white towelling, between it and the warmth of her skin, hidden in the scented, secret valley of her cleavage.

'Liam!'

His name was just a sigh, forced out from her in the moment that her whole body froze, her entire being centred, or so it seemed, on that one small, burningly intimate point of contact between them. The point where all he had to do was make one tiny movement—either out and away *upwards*, leaving her skimpy protection secure and intact—or up and away, *towards* his chest, taking the towelling with him, breaking the weakening knot once and for all.

And still he waited.

'Liam!'

It was more impatient now. Very definitely a protest. The smile grew, became a wicked, beguiling grin that he knew she must feel against her cheek. They were so close, so very close.

'Yes, sweetheart?' he murmured softly, and saw her deep blue eyes fly open at the calculated provocation of the word.

He met the indigo burn of her gaze head-on, fixing and holding it so that there was no way she could look away, look anywhere but directly into his eyes.

'Our truth,' he said, low and huskily, and saw the surrender in her eyes before she even had a chance to open her mouth.

'Our truth,' she whispered on a note of submission, a note that yielded the victory to him—at least in this battle, if not the entire war.

And for Liam it was enough. It was all that he had been waiting for. If he was honest with himself, he couldn't have held out for a moment longer. The force of his desire was like a fire in his blood, the ache in his loins threatening to drive all hope of control from his mind, push him into the sort of wild behaviour that left no room for thought or consideration. And it took every last trace of control that he possessed to kiss her just once more before he made the movement they had both been waiting for.

Up and away, *towards* his chest.

A twist, a tiny tug, and the white towelling fell to the floor, pooling on the carpet at their feet. In the same instant the soft, heated weight of her breasts tumbled free and he held them securely, one in each of his hands, the whiteness of her skin shocking against the darker tones of his fingers.

The truth, Peta thought, adrift on a sea of wanting. Of need.

*Our* truth.

The truth was that they couldn't keep their hands off each other. Hadn't been able to from the start, and still couldn't now. And so she had known that as soon as he touched her she was lost. That the wild, primitive pin-pricks of fire that started all over her skin would swiftly merge into one total, blazing conflagration that would take control of her, leave her totally at its mercy. And when he kissed her she felt the response deep inside, where everything tightened, tensed, woke to stinging need.

His hands against her breasts and the touch of his mouth on her skin was turning her blood molten, making it pound fiercely in her veins. All the fears, all the doubts of the day, of only moments before, had evaporated, burned up in the blaze of heat inside her.

'Want me?'

It was a low, husky whisper against the curve of her ear, his breath feathering against her skin. And as he spoke his hands were working a wicked, tormenting magic, thumbs describing tiny, erotic circles over the delicate surface, moving closer and closer to the tight pink nipple, making her shiver in convulsive delight.

'Want me?' he said again. And when she didn't answer he punished her by closing a finger and thumb over each straining bud, tugging softly until she moaned aloud in a conflict of rebellion and abandonment.

'Peta?'

'What do you think?'

She was incapable of answering in any other way. Incapable of hiding her feelings from him. Incapable of pretending she felt anything more than the yearning, demanding hunger that had uncoiled deep inside her and was throbbing uncontrollably, low down in her body.

'I think...'

There was a tremor in his voice that revealed the struggle he too was having to keep control over his powerful physical feelings.

'I think that I'm wearing rather too many clothes for this. Why don't you help me out of some, hmm?'

And when she turned faintly confused, passion-blurred eyes on him, frowning in an effort to drag her thoughts back from the erotic paths they were following, he grinned and then kissed her again, tugging his tie free at his throat as he did so. Discarding the sliver of silk somewhere over his shoulder, he lifted Peta's hands, laid them on his chest, just on the button band of his shirt.

'Help me...' he whispered again.

But this time Peta needed no further urging. As soon as her fingers touched the soft linen of his shirt, felt the heat of his skin, the hardness of bone, the power of muscle, she was suddenly in the grip of a desperate hunger. She knew she couldn't rest until she could touch him, really touch him. Until she could feel his body without the barrier of any form of clothing between them at all.

And so she fumbled and wrenched at the small, pearly buttons, snatching them open, tugging, until one finally spun away to land with a small clatter somewhere on the nearby dressing table.

But neither Peta nor Liam saw it go. Or cared where it fell. They were both intent on getting rid of as many clothes as possible, as quickly as possible, no thought for anything else.

Liam had already kicked off his shoes, yanked open his belt. He paused only for a moment as Peta slid down his zip, peeled the elegant trousers over his hips and down the muscular length of his legs. Even as he freed himself from their clinging coils round his ankles she had made her way back up his body, hooking her thumbs into the sides of the black shorts, easing them away from the heat and pressure of his fierce erection.

Liam's breath hissed in again sharply and he froze instinctively. The instant reaction made Peta bold, erasing all the insecurity and the uncertainty that his earlier negative response had created. Pausing mid-movement, she looked up at him, blue eyes gleaming, a provocative smile tilting the corners of her mouth.

'No?' she teased, making as if to undo her action and let the fine cotton fall back into place.

'You dare!'

Liam's voice was low and rough, thick with the hunger that had scored two streaks of colour along his broad, slanting cheekbones.

'You witch!' he added even more rawly as she still hesitated, delighting in the power she had to reduce this big, strong, and normally totally self-contained man to this state of yearning need.

'So now I'm a witch, am I?' She laughed, never taking her eyes from the darkness of his. 'Well, if that's the case, then perhaps I should put you under a spell.'

'You already have, and you know it! Peta...'

His control was slipping fast. And, if he only knew it, so was hers. Her pulse was pounding so hard that her head felt light, her thoughts swimming. She wanted to take his mouth again, to taste him on her lips, on her tongue. She wanted him to enfold her in his arms, to take her down onto the bed with him, cover her with the hard weight of his body, fill her, take her—take her with him to the fulfilment they both knew was the inevitable, the only end of this shivering excitement.

And yet, at the same moment, she wanted to delay. Wanted to hold onto this thrill of anticipation for as long as she could, so that that fulfilment, when it came, would be beyond anything she had ever known before.

But, even as she hesitated, Liam took matters out of her control. Capturing her wrists in his hard grip, he held both of them prisoner easily in one hand while his other arm scooped her up off her feet and swung her over onto the bed, dropping her down onto the softness of the covers. While she was still recovering from having her breath snatched away by the suddenness of his response, he dispensed with what little remained of his clothing and came down beside her, pulling her roughly towards him.

'Tease me, would you, you little witch?' he muttered, imprisoning her beneath him and pushing strong fingers into her hair, dragging the dark silk back from her flushed face. 'Make me wait?'

His mouth crushed hers fiercely then danced away

again, tongue and teeth tantalising her skin, stroking, tasting, nipping at the softness of her earlobes.

'Well, I'll show you what teasing's really like. How it feels to want someone so much that you feel you'll die if you don't have them. That your head will burst, that your heart will stop beating. I'll make you ache with needing me, bring you to the point where you won't care if the world ends—because you won't even notice it happening. All you'll care about is that I'm here, with you—in you! You won't want to know about anything else. Oh yes, I'll *show* you, lady!'

Deep inside, Peta shivered, her whole being seeming to turn to jelly. She had no doubt at all that he could do everything he had promised. All that and more. And she could only lie there, waiting, wanting everything he could give.

It wasn't as if they had never made love before. A year together had given them knowledge of each other's bodies and all the secret pleasure spots that each of them possessed. It had created an understanding of how they both felt, how they reacted, what they liked and what they wanted. When to touch lightly, softly, gently and when to increase the pressure of a caress or the urgency of a movement until it was not just a stroke but more a demand without words.

But this time it was as if everything Liam did had a new skill, a new sensuality. Within seconds of his whispered threat Peta was quivering under his hands, reduced to a shameless, abandoned wreck of hunger, only able to express her need through moans of delirious abandon. Several times she moved her restless body against his, yearning, pleading, seeking the ultimate fulfilment of his possession, only to have him shake his dark head in refusal and subject her to even more erotic torture. Only at last, when she was sure that she would die if he didn't take her *now*, did he move over her and consummate their lovemaking with one wild, fierce thrust of his body.

It seemed to Peta that the world splintered around her even in those first few seconds of possession. There couldn't be any more pleasure, her whirling mind told her. Or if there could, then she couldn't cope with it.

It only took a few seconds to learn that she was wrong on both counts. There *was* more, and in spite of feeling that she would split apart if she experienced it she now realised that it had only just started. Her blood singing in her veins, her pulse throbbing, she met and matched every forceful movement Liam made, gave back kiss for kiss, caress for caress, demand for demand. Between them they rode the wild, blazing waves of passion, each time going higher, higher, higher, until at last there was nowhere else to go. The summit had been reached, the peak of passion scaled, and, with each other's name escaping in a hoarse, shaken cry, they tumbled over it and down the far slope into oblivion.

# CHAPTER THREE

PASSION was what their marriage was built on, Peta told herself as she watched Liam dancing with one of her friends later that night.

The spectacular ballroom of Hewland Hall was brilliantly lit by a dozen glorious crystal chandeliers. In the far corner of the huge room, an enormous Christmas tree reached almost to the ornate ceiling, and red, gold and green garlands festooned the walls. It was a gorgeous, wonderful scene, but all she was conscious of was the tall, powerful figure of her husband.

A smile curved her mouth, her eyes becoming darkly dreamy as she recalled how it had felt to be in his arms just a few minutes before, the way he had held her close to the heat and strength of his body, his cheek pressed against hers.

Passion was what had pushed them into the marriage of convenience that had suited them, and pleased both their families. The sort of passion that had consumed the two of them in its fires earlier, so wild, so all-powerful that even now she could still feel her blood heat and her skin tingle just to think of it. The sort of passion that was so overwhelming that it couldn't be denied. It had brought them together, held them in thrall for the past year, and had seemed so overpowering that, in the absence of any other, stronger feeling, it had seemed enough to hold them together for as long as they wanted.

Passion and the longing for children.

The smile left her mouth abruptly, leaving her face looking bleak and pale. All her life she had dreamed of becoming a mother She had enjoyed her work as a PA, knew she'd been good at it, but a child—children—of her own had always been at the centre of her thoughts. So it had come as something of a shock to her to find that, at twenty-six, almost twenty-seven, she was not only not yet a mother but also still single, without even a fiancé, or yet a boyfriend on the horizon. The fact that her brother, three years younger, was already the father of a two-year-old boy, with another child on the way, had only added to her feeling of emptiness, the yearning to have a family of her own.

And it had to be a family. She didn't want to be a single mother. A child had the right to two parents who loved and cared for it, and she was determined that her baby would have the best she could give it. So when Liam had told her how much he wanted children too, it had seemed like the perfect answer.

But then she had had to go and ruin things completely by falling in love.

Her hands closed over the long skirts of her midnight-blue dress, crushing the fine velvet dreadfully. This hadn't been on the cards. Hadn't been part of the bargain they had agreed between them.

'But what happens if this isn't enough?' she remembered asking Liam when he had first made the suggestion that they marry for lust rather than for love. 'What if one of us meets someone else? Falls for them…?'

'Falls in love?' Liam had finished for her, when she'd hesitated. 'You said you didn't believe in it.'

'I said I didn't know what it meant! And I don't. I've never known that sort of devastating, irresistible feeling for anyone. Never felt that without a certain someone in my life I would want to die, that my existence wouldn't be worth having. I've never experienced it and I'm not sure that I ever will.'

She had now, Peta thought wretchedly as her clouded blue eyes followed Liam around the dance floor, hungrily absorbing the lean, powerful lines of his body in the superbly cut dinner jacket and gleaming white shirt. She knew that feeling all too well, and didn't know how to handle it.

She couldn't drag her gaze away from this man who had been her husband for the past twelve months, and yet, in many ways, was still a total stranger to her. The subdued elegance of the classic black and white suited his tall frame to perfection. The fit of his jacket emphasised the broad, straight shoulders, the width of his chest and long, long legs under the fine fabric of his trousers.

In the light of the huge glittering chandeliers that hung from the high ceilings of the ballroom, the rich chestnut of his hair gleamed and shone, the copper lights in it seeming to catch fire and burn spectacularly. And the dark green of his eyes had the glimmer of polished jade, deep and impenetrable.

Those stunning eyes had looked just that way when she had asked him that question on the night before their wedding. When she had raised the possibility of one of them falling for someone else.

At the time she had felt that she had to broach it, just so that there was no possibility of a problem cropping up later, one that they couldn't handle. And it had been Liam that she had foreseen might find himself in love with someone else. After all, out of the two of them he was the one who had had some experience, however brief and unhappy, of the feeling that the world called love. The woman he had adored had walked out on him when he was twenty-three, and since then there had been no one, no single person that he'd felt more than a passing fancy for. Nothing that came anywhere close to love.

She had never expected that *she* would fall a prey to

that elusive emotion herself. And least of all that she would feel it for the man she was married to.

'We'll tackle that when we come to it—*if* we come to it,' Liam had said. 'But I don't think it's likely—do you? After all, it's not as if we're both naïve adolescents who don't have enough experience of life to know what we're doing.'

She felt like a naïve adolescent right now, Peta reflected wryly. Like some newly sexually awakened teenager, launched on her first major crush on the opposite sex. Thoughts of Liam crowded every second of her waking day. Dreams of him filled her nights. Heated, erotic, sensual dreams that had her waking restlessly, her heart throbbing, her breath ragged, and her skin so damp with perspiration that she felt sure that Liam, sleeping peacefully at her side, would sense it and, waking, want to know the reason for it.

In the beginning, in the days when passion had been all that held them together, she wouldn't have had any trouble in telling him how she was feeling. She'd done it more times than she could count, reaching for him and entwining her arms around him to draw him closer. She had pressed her mouth to his, tangled her fingers in his hair, holding her body against the hard length of his, coiling long smooth limbs around his equally naked, hair-roughened ones.

'I want you,' she had been able to whisper to him then. 'I want you more than I can say. I want you to make love to me—want you inside me—and I want it now!'

Then, passion had made her brave, need had made her forthright. She had been totally direct about her feelings because they had been that basic, that uncomplicated. But as her emotions had changed, so had her approach to this husband of hers.

*I love you* was just three little words—no more, no less

than *I want you*, but so much harder to say. Impossible to say when she knew that they were the words Liam didn't want to hear. The last thing that he wanted to hear from her. The last thing that he could offer her in return.

And so she had kept silent, and that silence had grown wider and deeper as the days and the weeks had passed. If it would have been difficult to speak at the beginning, it would be impossible to break her silence now. She had grown so accustomed to hugging her secret to herself that she knew the words would shrivel on her tongue if she so much as tried to express them. It was easier to keep silent. But keeping silent had also meant keeping her distance, and she knew that Liam had noticed her withdrawal. How long would it be, she wondered, before he started to question the reasons for it?

'Penny for them?'

The softly spoken question jolted her from her memories with a start, dragging her back to awareness of the fact that the music had stopped. The dance had ended, and her husband and friend had come to where she was standing at the side of the room, Liam's arms snaking round her waist and pulling her close with a casual possessiveness that made her heart thud high up in her throat.

'For—for my thoughts?' she hedged awkwardly, playing for time. It was a struggle to speak, to ignore the warm weight at her back, the knowing hand that rested on her hip, blunt fingers splayed out over the curve of her buttock. 'They're not worth much. Not even a penny, really.'

'I don't believe you.'

It was Stephanie, her friend, who spoke, laughter warming her voice.

'I saw the way you were looking at us just now, watching every move we made out there on the dance floor. And I don't kid myself that it was admiration for my dancing that held you spellbound in that way. Or that you were envying my dress—not considering that lovely creation you're wearing!'

'Well, thank you.'

Peta bobbed a laughing curtsey, hoping against hope to distract her friend from the path her thoughts were following. She knew that that narrow cut of the deep blue velvet dress suited the slender lines of her figure, and that the sleeveless, tight-laced bodice revealed the creamy skin of her shoulders and arms, the beginnings of the curves of her breasts, the shadowy suggestion of the fullness of her cleavage.

'So I suspect it was the person who gave you that spectacular necklace who was really in your thoughts. I take it that was an anniversary present from Liam?'

Peta's fingers went instinctively to touch the brilliant diamond necklace that her husband had fastened around her neck just before they'd left for the party at Hewland Hall, his grandfather's home. She had swept her dark hair up at the back of her head, exposing the full length of her throat and neck, so displaying its beauty more effectively, while at her ears sparkled matching earrings which he had given to her only that morning.

'Yes, Liam gave it to me.'

'I must say that this husband of yours has excellent taste.'

'But of course.'

Liam's arm tightened possessively around Peta's waist, tucking her up against the warmth and strength of his body.

'I chose Peta as my wife, didn't I? We're the perfect combination of breeding and money.'

He made it sound like a joke, and clearly Stephanie took it that he meant it flippantly, but deep inside Peta felt something twist sharply at the thought that in fact he had spoken nothing but the truth. The Hewland family, whose only daughter Liam's mother had been, were long-established landowners in the county. But by the standards of her own family, they were newly wealthy. The Lassiters could trace their ancestry back to the Norman Conquest, but as a result of too many death duties and some desperately unwise speculation on the Stock Exchange they were cash poor.

That was why her parents and Liam's grandfather, who had been friends for years, had come up with the idea of a marriage that united their two families. That way, they'd reckoned, they would have the best of both worlds.

'Breeding?'

A new masculine voice took up the conversation. Tony, Stephanie's husband, had joined them, catching the tail-end of Liam's remark.

'Who's talking about breeding? Liam—Peta—have you got some news we should know? Or has my wife been letting you in on our little secret?'

'News? No.'

Peta answered hastily, looking anywhere but into Liam's face. She could feel the colour ebbing from her own cheeks as her conscience stabbed at her painfully, reminding her of the deception she was practising on her husband. It didn't matter that she had very good reasons for doing so. Liam would never see it that way. He wouldn't understand her motives; the way things had changed so much since she had realised just how she really felt.

'N-no—no news.'

'But we have!'

Stephanie didn't have to explain just what her news was. It shone out of her eyes, was there in the glow in her face, her smile. Peta's stomach lurched painfully. Her friend had been married only half as long as she had. Just six months ago she and Liam had been guests at Stephanie and Tony's wedding, and now her friend was announcing the fact that she was pregnant.

'Congratulations, Steph!'

She made herself say it, praying that her hurried move-ment forwards to hug her friend, the way that her face was muffled in Stephanie's tumbling blonde hair, would explain the catch in her voice, the jerky unevenness of the words.

She'd married Liam to have children. But as her own feelings about her husband had changed, so had her thoughts on bringing a baby into this marriage. And now here, right in front of her, was the image of exactly why she had felt forced to take the decision she had. Stephanie and Tony were so obviously deeply in love. They were a *couple* in a way that she and Liam could never be, the sort of parents that she dreamed of providing for her own child when the time came.

'That's wonderful news.'

She couldn't even make it sound genuine, Liam re-flected bitterly. Oh, perhaps someone who didn't know their private background might be convinced. They might actually just take the words at face value and not hear the bleak emptiness that threaded through them, draining them of any real warmth and delight. But to someone who was as sensitive to everything about this woman as he was, it was obvious that her heart wasn't fully in her re-sponse. That there was something at the back of it, throw-ing a dark shadow over her happiness.

And she wouldn't even look him in the face. Couldn't meet his eyes. Ever since he'd made that damn stupid remark about breeding she had been avoiding him quite obviously.

He could have bitten his tongue off as soon as he had said it. It had come too close to the truth. To the sort of dynastic marriage their families had wanted and that, at first, they had both been so determined to resist. He had trampled right in, reminding her of one of the reasons—apart, of course, from fancying the pants off each other so that they couldn't keep their hands, or other parts, to themselves—for their union. And now Stephanie had reminded her of the fact that he had failed to deliver on his promise.

Luckily at that moment the announcement of the fact that supper was being served proved a very welcome diversion. For once he was grateful that the formality his grandfather insisted on for these occasions meant that he and Peta, as the guests of honour at this event, had to lead everyone else into the dining room where the elegant buffet meal was laid out.

'What can I get you?'

'Oh—anything—I'm not really hungry.'

She still seemed distracted. Still wouldn't meet his eyes.

'Okay, then—you go and sit down and I'll bring you something over. I think I know what you like.'

Did she have to look so relieved to be given the chance to move away? It was obvious that she had chosen a table on the far side of the room, where she could sit on her own, away from everyone else. People would be thinking that they'd had a row—not the best possible image to present on their first anniversary, particularly not when they wanted everyone to believe that theirs was a successful, happy marriage.

'What's up with that pretty wife of yours, then, my boy?'

Joshua Hewland's tones sounded gruffly behind him, making Liam wince inwardly. He supposed that compared to his grandfather's eighty-two years just turned thirty must seem young, but he had never quite adjusted to the way the old man kept referring to him as 'my boy'.

'Nothing's wrong. She's just a little tired, that's all.'

'Tired?' Joshua's response was a blatant snort of disbelief and disapproval. '*Tired!*'

The old man's watery blue eyes looked sceptical and the glance he turned in Peta's direction was frankly disapproving.

'Tired! At her age! Young people these days have no stamina! Why, when I was—'

Abruptly he came to a halt and Liam groaned inwardly as he saw the disapproval fade and a newly speculative expression take its place.

'Unless, of course… Do you have something to tell me?'

Ruthlessly Liam squashed down the angry retort that rose to his lips. Telling his grandfather that it was none of his business was not the way to handle this, even if it was the reply he most wanted to give. Joshua's obsession with the Hewland line, the inheritance of the great house and the acres of land that went with it, was positively feudal. It was something that Liam normally respected, something he partly shared, but right now it touched on a very uncomfortable spot indeed and was not something he wanted to talk about, particularly not in such a public place.

'When and if we do have ''something to tell you'',' he declared stiffly, 'we'll tell you in our own good time and not before.'

His grandfather wasn't pleased. The way the thin old mouth clamped into a tight, hard line made that only too clear. That and the way his bristling white brows drew together in a disapproving frown.

'Well, don't mess about with this, lad!' he ordered brusquely. 'I'm not getting any younger and I don't have many years to waste waiting for you to provide me with an heir.'

'Don't you mean a *legitimate* heir?' Liam snapped back, anger flaring almost out of control.

It had been impossible to come to terms with the way that his grandfather had never fully accepted him, and when the old man harped on about having an heir to Hewland Hall it simply drummed home the way that Joshua was prepared to dismiss the fact that he had once had a daughter. Liam's mother. But Anna Hewland had offended her father's old-fashioned principles by having a baby and not even staying with, never mind marrying, the father.

'At least this child will be born into a legal marriage,' Joshua returned coldly. 'Though of course that wouldn't matter if only your mother had had a child by the man who had the decency to put a ring on her finger.'

'But she didn't,' Liam growled. 'And so you're stuck with me.'

As his stepfather had been, he reflected bitterly, recalling just how plain his mother's husband had made it that he resented having to support Anna's bastard child while she'd given him none of his own. Nigel Hastings had made his stepson's life a misery from the moment he had married Liam's mother, doting openly on the son and daughter he had brought with him from his first marriage and making sure that Anna's child had felt very much lower than second-best.

'Believe me, Grandfather, I want a child from this marriage every bit as much as you do.'

More, perhaps. As a lonely, unwanted adolescent he had escaped into dreams of his own home, his own family, a baby that was truly *his*. When his turn came to be a parent, he had vowed to himself, he would be the best father he could possibly be, erasing all the emptiness of the past in the warmth of his relationship with his child.

'I want to hold my great-grandchild in my arms before

I die,' the old man stated flatly. 'What's so wrong with that? What're you doing, lad? Firing blanks?'

*Hell!*

It was meant to be below the belt, he knew that. But the fact that it hit home with more cruelty than Joshua had been aiming for was solely down to the thoughts that had been running through Liam's head for weeks. The private fears that had nagged at him in his lowest moments.

Clamping his mouth tight shut, he bit back the savage retort that almost escaped him, concentrating fiercely on pouring himself and Peta a glass of wine and adding them to the tray on which he had already placed the plates of food.

'I'm working on it,' he growled furiously when he felt able to speak without exploding. 'Believe me, if I have anything to do with it you'll have that great-grandchild of yours by this time next year.'

He'd almost given himself away there, he thought cynically, cursing the display of temper that had somehow escaped even his ruthless control. It had alerted his grandfather's suspicions. He could almost feel the old man's gaze burning between his shoulders as he made his way across the room to where Peta sat.

She did look rather washed out, he thought. Unusually pale, and, now that he studied her more closely, there were faint shadows under the beautiful eyes. Shadows that the skilful application of make-up hadn't quite concealed.

Under the elegant jacket and shirt his heart gave a sudden jolt, thudding against his ribs as a sudden suspicion slid into his head. Was it possible...?

'What did your grandfather want?' was her first question, as he had known it must be. But at least this time he was prepared. He'd been imagining things earlier, he told himself privately. There couldn't be anything wrong.

He didn't feel as if there was anything wrong. And, if he'd read the signs right, then maybe Peta had news for him that would put all his concerns aside once and for all.

'Oh, just to congratulate us.'

He had himself almost back under control now. His tone was as even as he wanted, the smile he directed into her eyes apparently easy and without a care. He'd guessed her secret, he told himself. All he had to do was to give her the opportunity to tell him.

'Congratulate?'

Peta had reached for her glass of wine but now she paused with it lifted just partway from the tray.

*Congratulate?* Just the thought sent tremors of shock running through her. Had Liam said something that had made his grandfather think his dearest wish was coming true?

'On our anniversary, of course.' He said it lightly enough, but suddenly there was a new note in his voice, one that hadn't been there before—and one that she couldn't begin to interpret properly.

'He didn't look congratulatory—if anything he looked annoyed. Liam?' she tried again when he didn't answer her, instead reaching for a bread roll and breaking it open roughly. 'Was he angry about something?'

Somewhere she'd overstepped some invisible line, crossed a boundary that she didn't even know existed. Liam didn't say a word but a sudden stiffening of his long body, the way the strong fingers tightened, a disturbing change in his eyes, all communicated silently the fact that he didn't want to answer the question.

Which of course only made her all the more anxious for him to do so.

'What did he say?'

For the space of a couple of uneven heartbeats she thought that he wasn't going to respond, and all the nerves in her body stretched taut in tension at the fear of just what he wanted to hide from her. But then suddenly Liam shrugged dismissively and lifted his clouded green gaze to her face.

'Not angry,' he said carelessly, dropping the mutilated roll and reaching for his own glass in turn. 'It was more that he was disappointed that Steph and Tony beat us to it in the baby stakes.'

'Ohh!'

Hastily Peta put down the glass that she had lifted to her lips; suddenly knowing that she couldn't drink from it. Not now. Liam's words had made her throat close over abruptly. There was no way she could swallow anything without choking desperately.

'It means that much to him!'

'I told you he wants an heir for this place. But you knew that when you agreed to marry me.'

And it had all seemed so much easier then. So much less complicated. But she hadn't been thinking straight.

She hadn't been thinking at all.

They had both known from the start that her parents and Liam's grandfather had been matchmaking with a vengeance when they had arranged for the two of them to meet. Peta had been away in America for five years, working in Seattle, and before that she had been at university, only coming home in the holidays. So she had only seen Liam once or twice, and then perhaps for a brief moment or two. The boy, and then the adolescent she had known vaguely, had grown into a dark and devastating man. One she had been instantly drawn to and one who, if it hadn't been for her parents' interference and manipulation, she would have been glad to get to know better.

'It was why he and your parents introduced us in the first place.'

Liam's tone of voice, the expression in his eyes, told

her clearly that he too was thinking of the way they had met, the part their elders had played in getting them together.

'They weren't exactly subtle about it, were they?'

She aimed for airy lightness and missed it by a mile. It still stunned her to reflect on the way that, meaning to deliberately sabotage the matchmaking plan and go their own free way, they had in fact fallen in with exactly what the Lassiters and old Mr Hewland had wanted, though in the end for their own private reasons.

'If they'd broadcast their plans on the Internet or announced it in the papers it could hardly have been more obvious.'

Liam's tone was as dry as his smile, but he had picked up his roll again and was methodically ripping it to pieces with a sort of suppressed violence that made her shiver inside just to watch it. She wished he would stop. That he would just stay still—anything other than this disturbing, worrying restlessness that was setting her teeth on edge.

'Do you ever wonder what might have happened if we hadn't agreed to that first date?'

That caught him up sharp, stilling the restless movement of his hands. And perversely, having wished that he would stop, Peta was now forced to wish that he had done anything other than freeze as he had. His immobility, his silence, were terribly unnerving, and the way his jade-green gaze locked with hers made her feel as if something cold and unpleasant had just slithered uncomfortably down her spine, afflicting her with icy pins and needles all over.

'All the time,' he answered at last. 'If we hadn't gone out together that time—if I hadn't kissed you—then we wouldn't be where we are now.'

They had only agreed to the date because it had been

easier than arguing any more. Having been bombarded for some weeks, first with a succession of subtle hints and then some far more blatant suggestions, they had had more than enough. It had been drummed home to them at that dinner party, and again at every possible opportunity, that they would look good together, that their union would be the perfect match, the joining of the two families just what everyone had dreamed of, until Peta at least had been ready to scream.

It was then that Liam had come to her with a suggestion that he had hoped would earn them a little peace.

'Why don't we just give them what they want?' he'd asked, the wry expression on his face, the hint of weary laughter in his voice revealing that he was as sick and tired of all this as she was. 'I'm not looking for marriage and neither are you, but if we agree to go out together once—just to see—then maybe they'll leave us alone.'

'It might work—but not for long. If we do go out then that will satisfy them for a while, but do you really think it'll take very much time before they're at our throats again—wanting to know if you've popped the question yet—when we're getting engaged—if we've planned the date for the wedding?'

'Ah, but that's where we fool them completely,' Liam had told her. 'One date is all we have—at the end of which we declare that this relationship is never going to work. That we can't stand the sight of each other—never want to see each other again.'

That had been the plan. But it hadn't worked out that way. Instead, life had turned the tables on them and they had found themselves unable to fight against the hand that fate had dealt them.

At the end of that first date Liam had taken her back to his house, on the edge of the Hewland estate, five miles from Hewland Hall, and he'd invited her in for coffee.

'We might as well do this thing properly.' He'd
laughed. 'After all, it's the one and only date we're ever
going on together.'

Which was a pity, Peta had reflected, because she'd
enjoyed the evening. She might even have been willing,
if Liam had suggested it, to accept an invitation to go on
another one. But coffee had been all that was on offer,
and so coffee was what she had agreed to.

And at the end of the evening, with the coffee drunk,
she had been about to go on her way again when Liam
had said, 'So we're agreed. We tried it once—couldn't
stand each other. And now we never want to see each
other again?'

It was going to be difficult to stick to that, Peta had
thought. Left to herself, she would have been happy to
see Liam again, even if she knew how both sets of families would interpret it. She'd even thought of suggesting
it.

But then, moved by some impulse of his own, Liam
had decided to kiss her goodbye. The kiss had been aimed
for her cheek, but at the last second she had moved and
instead it had landed squarely on her mouth. And in the
moment their lips had met the resulting explosion of sensuality had meant that they both stopped thinking and
started reacting.

It was as if they had been caught up at the heart of
some whirlwind of desire that swept them off their feet,
lifted them high out of reality and hadn't let them go again
until they were exhausted and replete. Peta had lost count
of the times that they made love that night, lost track of
the hours that had slipped away in the heated world of
their mutual delight in each other's bodies. She had only
known that when at last, slowly and languorously, she'd
come back to any sort of thought, it was already the next
morning and way, way too late to convince anyone that
they felt nothing at all about each other.

# CHAPTER FOUR

THE clock was striking three in the morning by the time Liam and Peta let themselves back into the house at last.

'I'm glad to be home!' Peta declared, easing off the cashmere wrap that had kept her warm during the short car journey from Hewland Hall and tossing it over the arm of the settee. Sinking down on to the soft gold-coloured cushions, she kicked off her high-heeled sandals with a sigh of relief. 'I'm worn out!'

'Are you sure that's all it is?' Liam surprised her by asking, a new and unexpected edge to his voice making her sit up sharply, eyeing him in consternation.

'Of course that's all there is to it. What else could there be?'

His shrug appeared to be casual, perfectly indifferent, but the way he was watching her was the complete opposite. The piercing gaze made her think unnervingly of a keen-eyed, hunting hawk, circling high in the sky, above its prey, just waiting for the right moment to pounce. And the thought of Liam pouncing made her shiver involuntarily.

'I don't know,' he said coolly. 'You tell me.'

'There's nothing to tell.'

'No?'

He crossed the room to where a cognac bottle and a couple of glasses stood on a silver tray on the highly polished wood of the elegant sideboard. To Peta's overly sensitised hearing the sound of the cork being pulled from the bottle seemed unnaturally loud in the quietness of the room. The only other sound was the faint hiss of the coal

49

fire, left banked up by the housekeeper against their late return. In the big bay window the lights on another giant Christmas tree, only slightly smaller than the one at Hewland Hall, flickered on and off, chasing each other in a display of patterns that normally she loved to see but which tonight she found grated on her tightly stretched nerves.

'Are you sure?'

Liam's attention was apparently concentrated on the measure of spirit he was pouring, but something about the tension in the long, straight back that was turned to her warned Peta not to rely on that impression in any way.

'Liam—what is this? Some sort of interrogation?'

'Only if you see it that way. Drink?'

He lifted the cognac bottle again and turned to her, one dark eyebrow lifting interrogatively. But at her shake of her head he set it down again with an expression on his face that tugged at something sharply, twisting her nerves in apprehension.

'That's…'

To her annoyance, her voice failed her, coming to a croaking halt, and she had to swallow hard to ease the uncomfortable dryness in her throat before she could continue.

'That's how it seems to me. Just what is it you want to know?'

'Anything you want to tell me.'

He was sure she did have something to tell him. After that first flash of suspicion, the conviction had grown on him throughout what had remained of the rest of the evening, and everything about her behaviour now confirmed it.

She hadn't said anything at the party, but then she hadn't had a chance to say anything. They had been interrupted several times over supper by friends and colleagues, and finally Peta's own parents had come to chat and offer their congratulations on their anniversary. Any opportunity they might have had to share a private moment had been lost and there had never been another one.

And Peta would want to tell him the news privately; he was convinced of that. After all, her longing to have a child, and his need to provide his grandfather with an heir, had been so much a part of the secret reasons why they had agreed to marry rather than simply have an affair after that first mind-blowing night of passion they had shared on their first date. She wouldn't want it broadcast, even if the party this evening might have seemed like the perfect opportunity to announce the good news.

And it was good news—the best. It would get his grandfather off his back once and for all—and it would put to rest the nagging fear that had plagued him as each month passed and still Peta hadn't conceived. With an effort he suppressed the grin that would betray the fact he'd spoiled her surprise by guessing too easily. If only she would stop messing about and tell him straight.

'I rather thought you had something on your mind earlier this evening—and again at the party.'

Coming to sit in the armchair opposite, he leaned back in apparent relaxation, cradling the crystal glass of fine cognac in his cupped hands. But once again it was the look in his eyes, the way their intently focused gaze was fixed on her face, that made Peta shift uneasily on the settee.

If she'd struggled to try and tell him the truth before this evening, now she lost her nerve completely. Call her stupid, call her a coward, but what she wanted most in all the world was to have this one night—the night of their first anniversary—free of the explosion she knew must inevitably follow if she told Liam what she really did have on her mind.

'I told you—there's nothing…'

'Nothing to say?' Liam repeated, his tone making it clear that he didn't believe her. 'Well, in that case this is going to be a rather dull conversation.'

Did he suspect something? Peta racked her brains, trying to think of some way she'd given herself away. Or was it something completely different? Had she made some mistake at the party? Talked to some man for too long? Was he—could he be *jealous?*

Her heart lurched into an unnaturally fast, sharp, staccato rhythm at just the thought. If she could believe that Liam was jealous, then surely that meant he felt something for her? Something that went deeper and further than the sexual passion she knew burned in him for her body.

It was scary just how much it meant to her even to think of that possibility, to realise just how much hope she pinned on even the tiniest sign that he might care more than he ever let on. She only knew that it was what she wanted most in all the world.

'I think I will have a drink after all,' she said jerkily, pushing herself to her feet before he could offer to get it for her.

At the sideboard, Peta rejected the idea of a brandy, opting instead for a long, cold glass of sparkling mineral water. Her throat was still parched, and besides she felt so painfully on edge that the thought of anything alcoholic didn't appeal. It would probably only add to the feeling that was buzzing uncomfortably around in her head.

Still standing, she gulped down half of the water before turning back to face Liam once more. The cooling effect of the water had eased her tension a little, made her feel confident enough to confront him.

'So just what is it I'm supposed to have done?'

Liam had been raising the brandy glass to his lips as

she spoke and he deliberately continued the action, swirling the amber liquid round and round and then taking a long, slow swallow before he spoke.

'Nothing,' he stated flatly, making her frown in renewed confusion.

'Nothing? Then what…?'

'It's not what you've *done*,' Liam inserted coolly, his eyes once more fixed on her face, watching the play of emotion across her expressive features, noting the bewilderment that clouded her wide blue eyes. 'More like what you've not done.'

Not done?

All of Peta's sense of relief evaporated as swiftly as it had come. What had she *not done*? What had she missed out on? Forgotten?

Was it something to do with their anniversary? She knew that Liam was totally determined that their marriage should appear to all intents and purposes to be a real one. They might have agreed to it being on rather unconventional lines, but that had been between themselves, and between themselves was how it was to stay. To everyone else it was supposed to be a love match. A happily-ever-after story in which both families could convince themselves they had played matchmaker in order to bring it about.

And she was sure that she had kept up her side of the bargain. Liam wore her anniversary gift of an elegant gold watch around his wrist. Several people had commented on it during the evening, and she had seen him showing it to her mother with every appearance of pleasure. A carefully chosen card stood on the mantelpiece, displayed for anyone who visited the house to see.

Peta bit her lip hard, blinking back the sudden burn of tears as she recalled how long she had spent deciding just which card to buy. She had found it a terribly black irony that even if she selected one that declared undying love and devotion, as she had wanted to, then Liam would never believe it. He would only see the flowery words as evidence of the part he thought she was playing, the role she had assumed to deceive the world while he alone knew the truth.

The knowledge made her voice high and sharp when, pushed into it by Liam's protracted silence, she spoke again.

'Well, are you going to tell me? Are you going to let me know exactly what—in your opinion—I've neglected to do? Or are you going to sit there throwing out veiled accusations all night long?'

'Not accusations,' he countered. 'I've been concerned about you.'

It was the last thing she expected.

'Concerned?'

She slumped back down on the settee, no longer knowing what to think. Concern was good, wasn't it? *Wasn't it?* So why did she suddenly feel more on edge than ever?

'Concerned about what?'

'The way you've behaved all evening. You've seemed on edge—not quite yourself. You hardly ate a thing at supper…'

'I wasn't hungry—'

'And you haven't been drinking.'

His dark eyes went to the cognac bottle and then back to the mineral water, still fizzing slightly in the glass in her hand.

'And your point is?'

She must be slow on the uptake because her mind couldn't connect the things he was saying to anything she thought she'd done. No, something he said she'd *not* done. What…?

And then, hard and fast as a blow, and just as shocking

in its impact, the truth dawned, rocking her back in her seat and making her hand shake so that some of the water slopped over the side and onto the rich blue velvet of her dress.

'Oh, no—no, not that! I mean—I'm not pregnant, if that's what you mean.'

It *was* what he'd meant; that much was obvious. And he was shocked—appalled—to find out how wrong he had been. It was stamped onto the stunning features, etching lines around his nose and mouth. And the moss-green eyes were suddenly clouded with shock, hard fingers clenching tight over his glass until she fully expected to see the fine crystal shatter under the pressure.

'Are you sure?'

When he had been expecting to hear the exact opposite it was impossible to take in, or even understand what he was hearing. It couldn't be true. He had been so very sure…

'Yes. I'm positive.'

'How positive?'

He felt as if he had received a blow in the chest, bruising it hard. His breath had been snatched away, leaving his lungs raw and painful, and his heart had jolted into a rough, uneven thunder that he could not get back under control.

'Totally positive! I'm not pregnant, Liam.'

'You can't be so certain…'

'Oh, but I can. I—'

Suddenly terrified at what she had been about to give away, she caught herself up sharp and clamped her mouth tight shut on the dangerous words.

*I know I can't possibly be pregnant because I'm on the Pill.*

The dreadful admission reverberated inside her skull, making her want desperately to shake her head to drive it away. But any false move, any unexplained action, would only draw his attention to her even more, and that was something she was frankly terrified of doing.

She had known that Liam wanted a child, but until she had seen his reaction this evening she hadn't understood quite how *much*. But the rawness of his voice, the blaze of shock in his eyes had told its own story. She didn't know why Liam had been so convinced that she was expecting his child, but it was obvious that he was devastated to discover that she wasn't. And, having seen that, she didn't like to anticipate what might happen if he found out that she had deliberately taken precautions to ensure that she didn't conceive.

'How do you know?'

'I—I know my own body Liam! If I was pregnant I'd be aware of it. There would be changes…I'd feel different…'

She was blustering now, on the defensive, and she knew it. And if she wasn't careful then he would see her near panic in her face and begin to suspect what she was trying to hide.

If he started to question, to probe into her reaction, she knew she wouldn't be able to hold out very long. For one thing Liam would very easily see through her careful cover-up and slice straight through to the truth. He was too incisive, too intelligent to be deceived for long. As it was, she was frankly amazed that she'd managed until now without him suspecting that something was up.

Her skin felt as if it was inflicted with stinging pins and needles, and, too nervous to sit still, she got to her feet, pacing restlessly to the window to stare out at the black, icy night.

'And you don't?' Liam shot at her. 'Feel different, I mean?'

'No…'

Reflected in the dark window in front of her, she could see an image of the lighted room, so she knew when Liam got to his feet and turned towards her, his glass still in his hand. The eerie gleam of the tiny crescent moon cast shadows on his face, making his eyes just deep, dark caverns above the colourless planes of his cheeks.

He had made no secret at all of the fact that what he wanted most out of marriage was a child—apart from the sex, of course. The sex they had both wanted. Wanted so desperately that they hadn't thought beyond the fact that marriage ensured they could share the same bed all night, every night, and no one, not even her disapproving parents or his old-fashioned grandfather, could interfere.

But she had hoped that from that desire something else would grow. She had dreamed, prayed that, like her, Liam would come to realise that this relationship meant so much more to him than just the blazing passion that had stopped him thinking straight. That he would want to make their marriage of convenience into such a real one that she would be happy—overjoyed—to have the baby of her dreams—and his—with him.

'No,' she said flatly, still watching his reflected face in the glass. 'No I don't feel any different at all.'

The *feeling different* had come months ago, when she had made the discovery that had changed her whole life. Before that she would have said that she too wanted a child more than anything.

But since she had come to realise how much she loved Liam everything else had shifted, the balance of her life totally altering—for ever.

'I wish I could say I did, but it wouldn't be true.'

She heard the sound of his glass crashing down on the polished wood of the mantelpiece and shivered inwardly, wrapping her arms around herself as if against the cold. But deep inside she knew that she was really trying to protect herself against the pain of knowing how she was deceiving him.

She could change this situation so easily, if she wanted. She simply had to forget all her fears, all her doubts, throw them away with her pills, and she could be pregnant in a few weeks—a couple of months at the most.

Or could she?

They had been together now for twelve months, and in that time she had lost count of the occasions on which they had made love together. The first three months Liam had surprised her by insisting on taking contraceptive precautions himself, until they settled in together, but every one of the months after that she had hoped, prayed that she might have conceived, only to have her dreams bitterly dashed as nature took its usual course.

It was only when she had realised just how she felt about Liam that she'd begun to wonder if her innermost thoughts had actually caused the problem. If her own insecurity in a marriage where she knew her love for her husband wasn't returned had in fact created a mental barrier to what she had thought she most wanted. That was when she had first thought about going on the Pill, until she could sort things out.

'I'm sorry, Liam.'

'Don't apologise.'

His voice was rough, harsh, scraping uncomfortably over already raw nerves, and the arms she had laced round herself tightened in instinctive response.

'It doesn't matter.'

That was so unexpected that it brought her swinging round, confusion darkening her eyes as they stared into his strongly carved face.

'You don't mean that—you can't…'

'Can't I?'

One hand tugged loose the bow-tie at his throat while

the wide shoulders lifted in a shrug that dismissed her protest as totally irrelevant.

'I think you'll find I can—and do—mean it only too well.'

He had been shocked to see just how upset she'd been at having to admit to him that she wasn't pregnant. He hadn't realised how much the waiting, the wondering every month if this time they had conceived the so much wanted child, had affected her. It was no wonder that when Steph and Tony had made their announcement earlier this evening she had gone white as a ghost. Remembering how she had been unable to look at him, he cursed his insensitivity in bringing up the subject tonight of all nights, on the anniversary of the day they had married, with the idea of creating a child uppermost in their plans for the marriage.

'It doesn't matter,' he said again, willing her to believe it.

'But when we married...'

'When we married I said I wanted a child to inherit Hewland's. I still do. But we can't force these things. I can wait.'

He almost convinced himself. But what mattered was that he convinced her. If his grandfather was already suspicious that there might be a problem, then he didn't want the idea even crossing Peta's mind. He had promised her a child as part of their marriage arrangement and, by God, he was going to keep that promise if it killed him. He refused to let the fear of never having a baby take root in his thoughts. It wasn't going to happen, he vowed. He would make damn sure that it wouldn't.

Okay, so if she wasn't already pregnant, then he knew just how to make sure she didn't stay that way. They'd made a good start earlier that evening; maybe she had already conceived from that explosive coupling and just didn't know it. Just remembering the stunning satisfaction of their lovemaking then made his body harden in savage demand, leaving him in no doubt that the process of fulfilling his ambition would be one he could enjoy very much indeed. And, with luck, by the time their next anniversary came around they'd celebrate as parents as well as husband and wife.

He made himself smile, saw by the look in her eyes that it had been at least half convincing.

'Not everyone falls pregnant as easily as Steph…'

With an unnatural effort he kept the words pitched at the casually relaxed level he had been aiming for, even though they stuck in his throat and had to be forced out before they choked him.

'But that doesn't matter. We have time on our side.'

'Do—do you mean that?'

'Of course. It's not the end of the world. And besides, not hitting the jackpot this time means we will just have to try again.'

He took a couple of slow, cautious steps towards her, careful not to startle her by any sudden movement. She had unwound a little, but she still looked as if one false move and she would panic, her head coming up and her eyes widening. If he frightened her he had the suspicion that she would whirl and run, fleeing from him like the nervous fawn he had once come upon in a clearing in the Hewland woods and had startled so much that it bounded away before he had quite realised it was there.

'We can practise a little more.'

His mouth curved at the corners, the wicked smile making her catch her breath sharply as she gazed into the smoky darkness of his eyes.

'And practising can be so much fun.'

# CHAPTER FIVE

ANOTHER few steps and he was right next to her. Close enough to touch.

Green eyes locking with blue, holding her still by the sheer force of his presence, he reached out and touched her cheek. Her response was immediate. Her head went back slightly, eyes half closing, and her lips parted to let out a single, soft sigh.

'Do—do we need to practise?' she managed, and the shake in her voice brought a smile to his lips.

'What do you think?'

Light as a breath, the question danced over Peta's senses, warming her blood and making her heart kick in her breast. The hand Liam had rested against her cheek moved softly, trailing a burning path down her face, her neck, touching the exposed curve of a breast for the briefest second. Peta's throat dried instantly and she licked her suddenly parched lips, watching Liam's darkened gaze drop downwards to follow the revealing movement.

'*I* thought we were getting quite good at things.'

The provocative tone, the deliberate, slanting glance she shot him, were like a bolt of electricity that sizzled through every awakened nerve, the tingling sensation of delight making him laugh out loud.

'But there's always room for improvement.'

They were back on familiar ground, Peta reflected. On the well-trodden, safe, path that could only lead one way and end up in once place—in their bed, making wild, passionate love.

No, not love.

The unwanted thought sliced coldly into her thoughts like a blade of ice, threatening to destroy the beginnings of sensual awareness, the lazy uncoiling of need that had started with Liam's smile. *She* would make love, but Liam, as always, would only indulge in his appetite for sex, feeling no other deeper emotion than that.

So could she go through with it? Could she take the little he had to offer and ask for nothing more? Could she continue with this simply physical love when her heart was crying out for an emotional response from him?

She had to. It was either that or nothing. She had played this game, put on an act that this was enough, for so many months now. Surely it would get easier the more often she did it. And besides, her body was already in the grip of the waves of heat that simply thinking about going to bed with Liam always awoke in her. Heavy, cloying waves, like thick, heated honey, that were filling her thoughts, clouding her mind, making it impossible to argue with herself.

'So what would you want to improve?'

'Well, there was that shower we missed earlier…'

'A shower! At this time of the ni—the morning? Liam…!'

But even in her own ears, her protest had no real conviction. And she knew from the slanting glance he shot her that Liam thought so too.

Oh, who was she kidding? She *wanted* this. Wanted it so much. She couldn't say no. Didn't want to say no. She could accept the limited relationship he offered her for herself. It was only when she thought about bringing a child into it that things got complicated.

'Do you think that all those people who waved us off tonight after wishing us a happy anniversary thought that we were going back to—to make out in the shower?'

'Don't you think that all those people who waved us

off tonight knew exactly where we were going—and why? And don't you think that that was precisely what they expected of us? Just as they expected it of us last year when we left our wedding reception and set out on honeymoon? They knew we were desperate to be alone, to get into bed together—and they were probably madly jealous of us as a result.'

Strong hands reached out, met in the centre of her forehead between her fine dark brows, then moved outwards in a soft but firm smoothing action.

'What are you doing?'

'Trying to erase the frown you've been wearing ever since we got home. No!'

His own brows drew sharply together as she puckered her forehead again in confusion.

'Stop right now,' he reproved. 'When you look like that no one would believe you were still a newly-wed. And we are really newly-weds, sweetheart. Apart from the fact that we've only been married a year—we do everything newly-weds do.'

Except love each other. Peta dropped her eyes so that he wouldn't see the stormy clouds in their depths, revealing how much the thought stung.

'You couldn't take your eyes off me this evening.'

That brought her gaze flying up again immediately, blue eyes clashing with green and surprising there a dark gleam of triumph and satisfaction.

'I…' Peta began in consternation at the thought that he'd noticed, but her stumbling protest earned her a smiling shake of his head in reproach.

'Don't get uptight about it, darling, I was flattered—and I'm sure the way your eyes followed me convinced anyone that the only reason we married had been for love. And as a matter of fact I felt exactly the same way about you. You look sensational in that dress. Like a queen—

regal and yet sensual at the same time. I couldn't drag my eyes away from you. Believe me…'

His voice lowered, dropped a sexy octave.

'I was hot and hungry with wanting you all evening.'

'I—I'm glad I was the sort of wife you wanted.'

'The sort of wife!'

Liam mimicked her words with a cynical mockery that made her wonder if her voice had really sounded so prissy, so tight and proper.

'Lady, you are the perfect wife. Every man there must have been jealous as hell of me!'

Abruptly he stopped, frowned faintly, but just as she was about to ask him what was wrong he flashed her one of his devastating, soul-shaking smiles.

'But there was one thing I was longing to do all evening.'

He tugged softly at her hair, where a dark curl had escaped from the elegantly upswept style, dangling down onto her cheek. His gaze fixed and intent, smoky with desire, he let the silken strand coil softly around one finger, twisting it into a loose ringlet.

'I wanted to get you to myself and unpin this sculpted creation, let your hair free to fall where it wanted…'

Suiting action to the words, he gently removed a couple of strategically placed hairpins, smiling his satisfaction as her hair tumbled down at one side, hanging wild and unrestrained over her face and onto the naked flesh of her shoulder.

'I wanted to feel it in my hands, run my fingers through it, have it brush against my face when I kiss you…'

Long, strong fingers slid under her chin, gently lifting her face to his. His kiss was slow, enticing, seductive, seeming to draw her soul out of her body and let it soar. And with her soul went all hope of rational thought, any attempt at trying to keep a grip on her feelings.

In the space of a single thudding heartbeat she went up in flames, the heat of passion raging through every nerve in her slender form. She didn't want to think; she only wanted Liam. And she wanted him with a hunger that was out of control, so that she trembled in his arms, grateful for the strength of their support that held her upright.

'Yes...'

The single husky word said that he knew what she was feeling, and acknowledged that he was feeling it too. His mouth captured hers again, plundering it, taking the surrender she was unable to hold back with all the physical arrogance of the conqueror.

And all the time his hands were busy in her hair again, pulling free the pins that held together the elaborate styling and discarding them carelessly on the thick carpet at their feet.

He had done just this on their wedding night, Peta reflected hazily. Then, too, he had taken down the hairdresser's skilful work, tossing aside the beautiful flowered headdress with as much carelessness as he now discarded the delicate hairpins. But tonight there was a new and slightly disturbing urgency about his movements, an unexpected roughness in the hands that tangled in her hair. He didn't hurt her but there was none of the calculated, almost lazy seduction of their wedding night. This Liam had spoken the truth when he had used the words 'hot and hungry' to describe the way he was feeling.

'Oh yes, my beauty, my wife. I know what you want and I want it too. I want to feel you naked against me. I want the scent of your skin on mine. I want to feel your hair on my body as I take you, let it lie like silk against my lips when I kiss your face.'

'Liam...'

His name was a choking cry of hunger, a shaken expression of the stinging current of need that was making her body twist and writhe in an agony of expectation. And each unthinking, uncontrolled movement brought her up against the hard reality of his strength, the powerful thrust of the hot desire that was potent as some elemental force, concealed but not in any way reduced by the civilised covering of his clothing.

Through the red cloud that hazed her thoughts she heard the faint sound of the long zip at the back of her dress sliding down, felt the sides of velvet fall apart as it slithered away from her to lie in an indigo pool around her feet.

'Oh, yes!'

It was a rawly indrawn breath, barely a whisper of sound on his lips. And his eyes were black with desire as they caressed every exposed inch of her body, slim and pale in the tiny slivers of material that were her only covering. The firm boning in the bodice of the velvet dress had meant that she needed no bra for support and her breasts tightened their rosy peaks in instant response to his burning gaze. Lower down, silk panties in the same colour as the dress and a suspender belt of feathery lace supporting the finest, most delicate of stockings were all that she had on.

'Yes, my wife…'

Liam swept a hand down the path his eyes had followed, making Peta quiver at the feel of his palm on her skin.

'Cold?'

Fiercely she shook her head, sending the newly loosened strands of hair flying around her face.

'No—oh, no!'

The shiver had been totally contradictory to the way she was feeling. Her exposed skin might have reacted to the touch of the cool night air, but deep inside she was all heat and molten passion. Her blood raced through in her veins, the heavy, throbbing pulse of desire setting up between her thighs and making her legs weaken beneath her.

She swayed towards Liam, but some change in her face had alerted him, some instinctive sixth sense where she was concerned. Immediately his arms came round her, lifting her off her feet. Supporting her at her back and under her thighs, he carried her towards the fire still burning in the grate and laid her down gently on the thick softness of the hearthrug.

'You needn't worry—I'll not let you get cold,' he promised her huskily, throwing off his clothes and coming down beside her even before she had time to miss the protective warmth of his presence. 'I'll keep you warm. More than warm.'

More than warm. She was there already. The cosy touch of the flickering flames bathed her flesh and the imprint of Liam's body was still against her, but it was inside where the deepest, most primitive heat of all smouldered, seething, just waiting for his enticement to burst into a raging inferno of need.

'But you're right. We do still have some room for improvement. No...'

His lips took hers in a searing kiss when she would have protested weakly.

'No, darling. You might think that I've made love to you before now—but that was nothing—*nothing* compared with what there is to come.'

He meant to take it slowly; he truly did. But seeing her lying there, with the light of the fire gilding the pallor of her skin, fine limbs splayed on the rug, the glory of her hair spread out around her head, he felt the fierce control he had imposed on himself start to weaken, fraying at the edges. He couldn't wait—he had to have her *now*. He had to take her, make her his, stamp his mark on her.

And then, surely—if the fates were kind—surely to-night he would set the seal on their bargain and impregnate her with the child they both wanted.

'Liam…'

His name was a whisper, soft as breath against his cheek, and as she spoke she lifted herself up from the rug and pressed her body close to his. The scent of her skin surrounded him, making his head swim. A wild pulse beat at his temples, pagan and erotic, and the pressure of her taut breasts against the frame of his chest was a sensual torment to his flesh.

'Liam…' she whispered again. 'Touch me—kiss me…'

And, blindly obedient, he did as she asked. He kissed—he touched—and as soon as he did, as soon as he heard her low, uninhibited moan, the red-hot tide that he knew was waiting swept upwards and over him, engulfing his thoughts until he was lost.

Peta had never known Liam so wild, so out of control. On every other occasion he had always taken the time and the care to make sure that she was as fully involved in their lovemaking as he was, that she was fully aroused before he went any further. But this time he was so totally abandoned to the sensual passion that had him in its grip that it was clear he had neither the control nor the thought to allow for such considerations.

Not that she minded at all. Even as he reached for her again she felt her own hunger rise to match his own. He had only to brush his hand over her skin, to press his lips to the quivering flesh of her body to start a raging conflagration of desire that seared along every nerve, scorching every cell in its path. Every touch, every caress, every kiss heaped response on response until she was clinging to him in mindless hunger, almost sobbing aloud in her need.

She welcomed the impatient urgency of his hands on

her breasts, the tiny, snatched; nipping bites he took at her skin, the force with which he held her close against him, almost crushing the breath from her lungs. Not since that very first time, when what had been meant as a good-bye kiss had instead sparked off the sort of overwhelming sexual hunger that nothing could assuage, had both of them been so completely out of control, so totally oblivious to anything beyond the demands of their bodies and the tornado of desire they had created between them.

'Liam...Liam...Liam...'

His name was a frantic litany of yearning on her lips and the uncontrolled movements of her body were deliberately meant to excite him, drive him further. She was lost, abandoned, knowing nothing but him, the feel of him, the scent of him, the sound of his raw breathing in her ears.

She caught his muffled curse as his uncharacteristically clumsy hands found the fragile barrier of silk that kept him from the intimate goal he sought. Heard the rip of the fine material as it was wrenched apart and discarded, the suspender belt and gossamer-fine stockings left ignored in the exigency of his need.

Powerful hands came under her hips, lifting her towards the potent force of his male passion, and her breath escaped in a high, keening sound of delight as he drove into her with a wild ferocity that obliterated all rational restraint.

Her body opened to him; her heart, her soul were his for the taking. She welcomed this new lack of control as evidence of the power of the ardour she had awoken in him. Surely if this wasn't love then it was something so very close to it that the difference couldn't be defined. Who had need of *words* when they could communicate in this most wonderful, most elemental of ways?

The strength of passion, the wildness, could not be

maintained for long. They were both so close to climax that it only took a couple of hard, forceful thrusts before it exploded around them. They cried out then, their voices chiming together, echoing in the stillness of the room for a moment, and then tumbling into silence as ecstasy deprived them totally of the power of speech.

It was the start of a long, erotic night. Peta had barely drawn breath after the wild assault on her senses that had been Liam's first lovemaking when she found that he had stirred at her side, reaching for her once more as the hunger resurfaced all over again. Though his impatience had eased a little this time, his ardour was no less fierce, and by the time he released her into orgasm Peta was a shuddering, mindless wreck, her face streaked with the tears of delight that had escaped from under her closed lids without her even being aware of it.

It was the nip of the night that woke them from the doze into which they had drifted a little later, the fire having burned out and the cool air chilling their sweat-slicked bodies. This time Liam gathered her up and carried her up the elegant, curving staircase to their room. Laying her on the bed, he came down beside her, sensing her shivering reaction to the sudden touch of the sheets.

But he had promised that he would not let her get cold. And he kept that promise, drawing her into the heat of his body, his touch stirring once more the aching need that only his possession could assuage. This time their intimacy was slower, languorous, each sensual delight drawn out to a point where she felt that her heart might actually break with the wonder of it all. She felt as if she was walking in the stars, whirling into the unknown spaces of the cosmos, losing herself entirely. And when the culmination of delight broke upon her it was as if her mind had shattered into a million, myriad fragments and she would never be whole again.

She slept after that, falling headlong into a deep dark pit of total exhaustion from which nothing could wake her, or the man who slept at her side.

Nothing, that was, until the cold, clear fingers of the late December dawn began to creep across the sky, warming it and brightening it so that the change in the light seeped under her closed eyelids. Disturbed, and suddenly, unexpectedly uneasy, Peta stirred and frowned, wondering secretly just what was wrong.

Because something *was* wrong. The warning lights in her thoughts told her that, the unexpected tension of her body, the twist of nerves in her stomach telling her to move. That now was the time for action.

Action on *what?*

The feeling seemed wrong. After the glory of the night, this morning she should feel complete, fulfilled—satiated. She was all of those. She was also worn out, lying in the warmth of the bed, close up against her husband's hard, lean form, her body limp with the aftermath of the storm of passion that had shaken it during the night.

But she also felt disturbingly unsettled, edgy, unnervingly rattled. And for no good reason that she could see or even begin to imagine.

'What?'

The sensation was so powerful that it pushed the whispered question from her lips as she turned over lazily onto her back, struggling to open eyes that had developed lids as heavy as lead.

Just what was wrong? Why did she feel as if she had swallowed something that lay weighty and uncomfortable on her stomach? And her throat was tight, as if she had tried to down a tablet only to have it stick halfway.

A *tablet!*

'Oh, no!'

Even as the exclamation escaped her she was half turning, her eyes flying open at last, all trace of sleep and relaxation fleeing as she checked fearfully to see if she had disturbed the man at her side.

Her sense of relief at the realisation that he hadn't moved, that she hadn't disturbed his slumber, lasted only a brief moment. Just long enough for the true reality of what she had forgotten to sink in and take deep, unwelcome root in her already unsettled thoughts.

A pill. *The Pill.* Last night, the tempest of sensuality and wanting had deprived her of the ability to think, and as a result she had totally forgotten to take her pill. And now it was...

Stretching out a careful hand, she turned the digital clock towards her and only just bit back the groan that almost escaped when she saw the time.

It was well over twelve hours since she should have taken it.

Moving so slowly that it seemed to her impatient mind that she barely made any progress at all, Peta slid from the bed inch by wary inch. Every sense alert to the tiniest sound, the faintest movement, she froze a dozen or more times when Liam stirred or muttered in his sleep. At every second she was terrified that he would awake and, missing her by his side, would want to know where she was, what she was doing. But somehow she made it to the floor and, snatching up her pale blue satin robe and wrapping it round her, crept silently into the *en suite* bathroom.

There was just enough light coming through the window so that she could see that her toilet bag was in one of the cabinets, where she always left it. It was as she pulled it out that something twisted harshly inside her, making her hand shake.

Was she doing the right thing? She had had her doubts before, but after last night the confusion in her thoughts was even greater.

'Liam?' she whispered. 'What's going on?'

It had seemed so easy at first. So uncomplicated. They both wanted children. Neither of them had any other relationship that they were involved in, no one to be hurt or even disturbed by the rather unconventional marriage they had planned between them. And the desire she had felt—they had both experienced—had been so potent that it had overwhelmed all other considerations. She couldn't live without this man in her life, in her bed, and it had seemed at the time that Liam had felt the same.

But what did he feel now?

Peta pulled out the turquoise-coloured bag and opened the zip top, then froze again.

What did either of them feel now?

She knew exactly the moment that she had realised she had fallen desperately in love with her husband of convenience. And the way it had happened had changed her perspective on everything once and for ever.

It had been on a terribly wet day at the end of August. After a rare long, hot summer, the drought had broken with a violent storm and savage downpours that had flooded the roads, blanking out car windscreens and making driving a desperately dangerous experience.

Liam had been out all day, involved in estate business. She'd known that he had to drive for miles, that his journey would take him on the nearest motorway, and she'd also known exactly when he was due back. So when, an hour and a half after the appointed time, he still hadn't appeared, and when the radio and television news had been full of a report of a multi-car pile-up, resulting in several tragic deaths, she had felt the first uncomfortable tremors of fearful unease.

Another hour and she had been in a state of total panic. Convinced that Liam was lying somewhere, injured or even dead, had pushed her into a state of such dread that she couldn't concentrate, couldn't focus on anything. And by the time he had returned home, with a tale of punctured tyres, a malfunctioning mobile phone and the inevitable hold-up caused by the tailback from the accident, she had been so overwhelmed with delight just to see him safe that she hadn't paused to wonder *why* she had felt so bad in the first place.

It had only been later, in the darkness of the night, that the truth had hit home with the impact of a bullet into her heart. And in the same moment had come a possible reason why she wasn't yet pregnant, as she'd dreamed.

The foil slip of pills was at the bottom of the bag and, sitting on the edge of the bath, she pulled it out with some difficulty then paused again, staring down at where it lay in her hand, unable to decide whether to proceed or not.

Liam had been so very different last night. His behaviour had been strange, alien for the controlled, guarded man she believed him to be. The man she had always known—at least, so far. A man who kept a strict watch on his feelings and rarely if ever expressed them forcibly. But a man who, last night, had been in the grip of a storm of emotion that even he couldn't hide.

Was it possible that, like her, he was coming to feel more than he had ever anticipated at the beginning of this marriage arrangement?

And, even if he was, would she be weak and totally foolish to consider even trying to describe that emotion as anything approaching *love?*

Once more she lifted the strip of pills, made to press out the one that she had forgotten to take the previous night, and once more she hesitated, unable to decide what to do. Closing her eyes in an attempt to be able to focus on the problem more clearly, she tried to sort out her whirling thoughts. She had promised Liam a child. A child—a legitimate child—was what he wanted from this marriage. As had she. And yet how could she balance her promise to him against her conviction of what was right for any child they might create?

'Peta?'

She hadn't heard any hint of movement. Hadn't caught the faint sound of Liam, stirring, waking, throwing back the bedclothes, coming to look for her. And yet now here he was, standing in the doorway right behind her.

Her eyes flew open just as the light flicked on, startling and half blinding her so that she dropped the slip of pills, which fell into the hand basin with a faint clatter that alerted Liam's attention. Stepping forward, he reached out a strong hand, caught up the pills and turned them so that the name was clear for them both to read.

Clear and sharply betraying.

'Liam…' Peta began, her voice cracking revealingly on the single word. 'I…'

But he wasn't listening. Instead his attention was fixed sharply on what he held in his hands, a fierce, terrifying frown drawing his black, straight brows forcefully together.

# CHAPTER SIX

'PETA!' Liam repeated, his tone growing darker, more dangerously ominous. 'What is this?'

'I don't…'

Oh, what was the point? Surely he could recognise the packaging? He must know!

'You can see what it is,' she muttered reluctantly.

'I can see, but I don't believe…' Liam retorted.

Didn't *want* to believe! his mind told him. Didn't want to accept that all this time, while he had been worrying himself stupid that he was failing—that his masculinity was in doubt—*she*…!

Anger was like an explosion in his mind, blasting away reason, totally destroying his ability to think straight. To think at all!

'Peta,' he growled even more savagely, the dark undertones of threat threading through his voice. 'What the devil is…?'

Peta had had enough. Getting to her feet in a rush, she whirled to face him, fighting against herself not to wince away from the black fury in those deep-green eyes.

'Oh, come on, Liam! You know only too well what you're holding!'

'Tell me.'

'Well obviously it's the Pill. The contraceptive pill!'

'*Your* contraceptive pill?'

'Who else's could it be?'

'And why—precisely—are you taking the contraceptive pill?'

'Why? You don't need me to tell you that, surely?'

'Maybe not. But I sure as hell need you to tell me why *you* are taking it. Why you've gone back on our agreement.'

'I...'

Bravado had got her this far, but bravado totally deserted her now. Looking into Liam's cold, set face, she felt her nerve shrivel up inside her. Her throat dried, and even swallowing hard did nothing at all to relieve the discomfort.

'I...' she tried again. And failed again.

At some point in the night Liam had pulled on a pair of black silky pyjama bottoms, but the broad, hair-roughened expanse of his chest was still bare. The memory of how it had felt to be in bed with him, to be held up close to the hard bone and heated skin of his powerful body almost destroyed her, leaving her despairing of ever getting an answer out. He was so close to her that she could see the faint marks on his skin, tiny reddened patches that indicated the lack of control in her responses to his potent lovemaking during the night, making her shiver in sensual recollection that threatened to destroy what little was left of her composure.

'You?' Liam prompted harshly.

'I d-didn't think the time was right for me to have a child. I—I wasn't quite ready.'

'You weren't quite ready?' he echoed dangerously. 'Now, correct me if I'm wrong, but wasn't it you who said that your biological clock was ticking—fast? That what you most wanted in all the world was a child?'

Yes, she'd said that, and at the time she'd meant it. Oh, who was she trying to kid? She still meant it! If anything she wanted that child more than ever because of who its father would be. The thought of bringing Liam's child into the world, of sharing this very special bond with him, meant more than she could ever say, especially now that she knew how much she cared for him. But she couldn't just think for herself. She had to take into account the possible baby's future, and that had changed everything.

'I changed my mind.'

'You changed your mind?'

Liam leaned back against the wall, the incriminating strip of tablets still gripped tightly in one hand.

'And when did you come to this momentous decision?'

'About four months ago.'

There was such a rush of relief in saying it. Relief at the thought that now it was out in the open. That she was no longer deceiving him. He would be furious—savagely angry—she knew that. It was inevitable; she'd been expecting it for months. And she'd brought it down on her own head.

But perhaps, just maybe, once he calmed down they'd be able to talk properly.

'*Four months?*'

'Yes, months! Are you going to repeat everything I say?'

Stony-faced, Liam ignored her outburst, persisting instead with his cross-questioning.

'So you've been on the Pill since—when?'

This time her nerve failed her completely and, unable to meet the blazing accusation in his eyes, she lowered her gaze to stare at the floor.

'Since September,' she whispered.

'What?'

She didn't know if he truly hadn't heard or if in fact he was simply determined to make her repeat it. To confirm the length and extent of her guilt.

'Since when?'

The way he rapped it out, the ice in his voice, was positively the last straw. Peta's dark head came up, tossing the length of her hair back over her shoulders as she did so.

The part of her brain that needed so much to tell him the way she felt about him was at war with the other, more cautious half. The half that warned her that the last thing Liam wanted was any precipitate declaration of love. Particularly not right now, when the expression on his face declared that she was the last person on earth that he wanted to have any claim at all on his emotions.

'Since September.'

Liam's hand clenched over the tablets in his grip, crushing the plastic brutally. The flare of fury in his eyes made her wonder if in fact he would also like to do exactly the same to her neck.

'And when, precisely, were you going to tell me?'

*Never*, his anger told him, the haze of fury blinding him so that he could no longer see her lovely face; those expressive blue eyes. Her lovely *deceiving* face. Her expressive *lying* blue eyes.

She had never intended to tell him anything. She had planned instead to keep him in blind ignorance, waiting and wondering, and growing more concerned every damn month.

Fury was like a red seething haze in his mind, making it impossible to see, impossible to think. Suddenly the confined space of the bathroom was too small to hold him. Too small to be in at the same time as Peta. He had to get out of here before he did something very very stupid. Very stupid and possibly very dangerous too.

'Liam…'

He barely heard Peta's voice through the buzzing inside his head. He couldn't even look at her, or pause to wait and learn what she had to say. He had to keep a hold on the temper that was boiling up inside him, threatening to spill over like lava out of a volcano, and pour down, destroying everything around him.

'Liam—what are you doing?'

Damn it, she was following him! Standing there at her side of the bed, looking at him as if he had gone mad. Well, perhaps she was right. Mad was just how he felt. Crazy. Wild. Totally out of control.

And all the time he had to keep his mouth clamped tight shut. If he opened it, let out a single word, then he would never stop. He would vent his fury on her in all the harsh, stinging words he could think of. And he didn't trust himself not to destroy her completely in his rage.

So instead he forced himself to concentrate on pulling on his clothes, every movement brusque to the point of violence. He wouldn't look her in the face for fear that the memory of how innocent she had looked, the ease with which she had deceived him, blasted apart his concentration.

'Liam…'

His breathed hissed in viciously through his clenched teeth. Couldn't she see what he was doing?

'I'm getting dressed,' he snapped with brutal succinctness, hoping that was it. But of course it wasn't.

'Why?'

Wasn't that obvious?

'Because I can't stand to stay here, in the same room as you, and not do something I may regret later.'

'But…'

'No!'

He had been wrenching up the zip on his jeans, bending to concentrate ferociously on the task, but he saw her movement towards him out of the corner of his eye and immediately he flung his head up, eyes blazing a warning to come no closer.

'Stay away from me, Peta. At this moment I don't trust myself where you are concerned.'

That stopped her. She hesitated, then froze, looking stunned. Her cobalt eyes even managed to cloud over, as if his reaction had actually managed to reach her—to hurt her. And yesterday, last night—five minutes ago—he might even have believed her. But now he doubted that he would ever believe a word that came from her lying mouth ever again.

'Liam—please—it doesn't have to be this way. I can explain—I always wanted to tell you.'

'Oh, sure you did!'

'But I did—I tried...'

For a second he almost believed her. The tremulous quiver to her delicious mouth almost deceived him, making him pause to reconsider.

But then it hit him. Thumped him right between the eyes so much that his head actually reeled back as if from the impact.

That was how she'd *always* distracted him. Her appeal to him was so strong that he didn't even think about their relationship. He just reacted. And reacted in the most basic, most primitive way that a man could, damn it!

His stomach curdled as he looked down at the messed-up bed once again, nausea rising in his throat. Inside his head, burning, erotic images of the night they had spent together played out over and over again, like pictures projected onto a cinema screen, until he felt sick at just the memory.

How long had she been playing him along like this? Since September or earlier? Had she ever really wanted the bargain they had made with this marriage, or had she had other, totally different reasons for going through with it? And, if so, what were they?

'Liam—please...'

'Liam—*no!*'

Peta blinked in shock at the force of his response, her heart twisting painfully as she saw the way he pushed his feet into his boots, stamped them down hard. He hadn't even responded to her attempt to explain. Instead he had just turned those hard eyes on her, looked straight through her as if she wasn't there.

And the frightening thing was that she suddenly felt she didn't know this Liam.

This wasn't the man she had met—charming, apparently easygoing, devastatingly attractive. Nor yet was he the Liam she had married. The sinfully sensual, provocatively arousing man who had only to touch her and she went up in flames like an explosive firework—light the blue touch-paper and stand well back. And he was certainly not the man she had lived with for the past year.

This man was none of those. In the space of a couple of heartbeats it seemed as if he had become someone else entirely. And this Liam was a hard, dangerous man. A man she couldn't reach in all the ways she had become so accustomed to using. A man who was only the space of a double bed away from her, but who might in fact be light-years distant, to judge by the burn of hostility in his eyes, the cold set of his stunning face.

'I want nothing to do with you.'

'But we should talk.'

'Talk? *Talk!*'

It was a harsh sound, a brutal explosion of rejection.

'Don't you think it's a little too late for *talking?* Isn't that something you should have done when you decided that you couldn't go along with our agreement? When you thought you'd go back on your word?'

'I didn't do that!'

'No?'

His dark head tilted to one side, a black brow lifting in

cynical question, his tone perfectly expressing his sardonic disbelief in her interjection.

'Then what exactly do you think you did?'

'I—I...'

What could she say? I lost my heart to you and as a result I just couldn't think straight? I was so deeply in love that I knew I couldn't go on as I was? I just couldn't have a child until I'd worked out exactly where I stood with you? I had to give myself a little time just to try— to try to get you to see what was happening to me, to try to win you round, get you to fall in love with me too?

Oh, he'd just *adore* that, really he would! The man who'd said right from the start that he didn't know what love was. Didn't believe in it. Who'd declared to her face that he truly believed that an arranged marriage could work out as well as—better than any—so-called 'love-match' because at least it had realism on its side, and neither of them was expecting something that no other human being could possibly provide. He wouldn't want to hear that she believed she'd fallen in love with him. Fallen so deeply, so irrevocably, so incurably, that she knew there could never be any other man for her in the whole of her lifetime.

'I—just delayed it a bit.'

'Of course you did, sweetie.'

His tone was pure saccharine, but saccharine dripping with poison, bitter acid that seemed to eat away at Peta's soul as the words fell onto her unguarded nerves.

'You "just delayed it a bit" so that—'

Abruptly he caught himself up, swallowing down the words he had been about to say.

'So tell me—were you ever going to let me know about this decision of yours?'

'Of course I was!'

'When?'

When?

Despairingly Peta thought of her original plan. Her original hope that one day, not too far into the future, Liam would find out that he too had fallen in love with his wife. Her dream that they could turn this arranged marriage into a real one and live happily ever after, as they did in all the best fairy tales.

She'd have had a baby with him like a shot then. But looking into his face now, seeing the black fury and total rejection stamped on the beautiful features, blazing in the brilliant green eyes, she recognised the dream for the vain, foolish delusion it truly was and shook her head sadly.

'No?'

Liam had caught the faint movement and pounced verbally with the speed and deadly intent of a hunting cat.

'Is that no, you won't tell me, darling? Or no, you never planned on telling me?'

'Of course I—'

'Of course! Of course?'

Liam echoed her protest with the sort of vicious accuracy that had her wincing in pain at the bite of his sarcasm.

'There is no "of course" about this, *sweetheart*.'

By the savage spin he put on the word she knew he remembered how she'd claimed that she didn't like being called that—and he meant her to remember too.

'From where I'm standing it seems to me that you started this marriage on a lie,' he went on, snatching up the nearest shirt and pulling it on with the sort of rough movements that made the fine material protest at such abuse.

'No—I never— I meant what I said...' she tried, but he ignored her and swept ruthlessly on.

'And for all I know you fully intended it to continue as a lie until...until...'

He was trying to fasten up the fine pearlised buttons on the shirt, and, uncharacteristically for Liam, was making a pig's ear of the job. Twice he got a button in the wrong hole, twice he pulled it out again with a muttered curse, and then finally, flinging up his hands in an expression of disgust, he simply gave up and let it hang loose, not even bothering to tuck it into the waistband of his jeans.

'Until what?' she forced herself to ask.

'Until you got what you wanted,' he answered with a careless indifference that turned the knife in her already wounded heart.

'And what do you think that was?'

'I don't know—you tell me. I can think of one obvious answer.'

'You can?'

It was more than she could do.

'What answer is that?'

Do you really need me to tell you? his expression said, scorn sparking like lightning in his eyes. But he answered all the same.

'Money,' he declared, brutally concise.

'Money!'

She couldn't believe what she was hearing.

'No way!'

'No? And why not?'

'Because—because—you just can't believe I'd do that! You can't believe I'd marry you—live with you—sleep with you—for *money!*'

She'd said exactly the wrong thing, she realised as she saw the dark scowl that twisted his handsome features. Or rather she'd said what she meant but in exactly the wrong way.

'I—' She tried to begin again, but already Liam was ignoring her, sweeping on unstoppably, totally ignoring her attempt at protest.

'What's wrong, sweetheart? Don't like to face the truth? Don't want to admit that you were prepared to come slumming if it meant marrying the heir to the Hewland fortune? After all everyone knows about your family—that the Lassiters are status-rich but cash-poor. You might be able to trace your ancestry back all the way to the Norman Conquest but you haven't got two brass farthings to rub together. This is what it's all about...'

Lifting one hand, he brandished it almost under her nose, rubbing the thumb and forefinger together in the gesture that was traditionally meant to symbolise miserliness.

'And that would be enough for you to be prepared to lower yourself far enough to become the wife of the bastard grandson of the richest man for miles around.'

'No.'

Once more Peta was shaking her head, but more desperately this time.

'No, it wasn't like that. Not at all.'

'No? Then why don't you tell me how it was? Nothing to say, darling?' he taunted cruelly, when she couldn't force her shock-paralysed lips to form any sort of answer. 'Cat got your tongue, sweetheart?'

It was the deliberate nastiness of that repeated 'sweetheart' that broke the frozen hold his words had on her ability to speak.

That and the way that Liam had looked away from her, coolly turning his attention to adjusting the sleeves of his shirt, folding back the cuffs to expose the sinewy strength of his muscular forearms.

It was the shirt he had worn last night, she realised. And couldn't help remembering how wonderful he had looked in it. How the stark black and white of his dinner jacket and shirt had contrasted so sharply with the burnished sheen of his hair, the emerald glow of his eyes. If she hadn't already been hopelessly in love with him, she would have fallen for him totally last night. No woman would have been able to resist him—no woman had, she reflected dully, recalling the sidelong looks, the flirtatious smiles she had caught being turned in her husband's direction during the evening. And Liam had smiled right back. He had flirted too, and danced with anyone and everyone, charming them all without the least tiny effort.

He could have had almost any woman there, too, if he'd wanted. And now, when she was least able to bear it, she recalled a phrase he had used once, in a rare, revealing comment about his estranged father—the man who had had a fling with Liam's mother and then fled, leaving her alone, pregnant and, in old Joshua Hewland's opinion, disgraced.

'My father was fickle as a tom cat,' he had said, bitter cynicism weaving its way through every word in the description. 'He spread his favours around without a care for anyone else's feelings. The year he spent with my mother was something of a world record for him.'

Like father like son. The phrase slid into Peta's mind with cold cruelty, making her shiver inwardly in fear. Like father like son? Was it possible? Could Liam, whose devastating looks had clearly come from his father's side of the family and not from his ash-blonde and grey-eyed mother, have also inherited William Farrell's fatal womanising gene? Did he share his father's inability to be faithful to anyone for more than a year?

The terrible thought and the fear it produced pushed her into a desperate outburst that she just couldn't hold back.

'Why don't *I* tell you how it is?' she flared at him, lifting her chin defiantly and tossing back her hair.

She welcomed the liberating rush of anger that swept the misery and despair before it, driving it away fast.

# CHAPTER SEVEN

'YOU sure you really want to know this?'

He was prevaricating, Liam admitted to himself, hedging deliberately, putting off answering until he knew what to say.

What *could* he say? Why had he married her? What was the *truth* after all?

The truth was that she had knocked him for six in the first moment he had seen her. That he hadn't been able to get her out of his mind. That he had known all about his grandfather's plans for his future—their future—and the way that her father at least had wanted to go along with it and he had been determined to sabotage the old man's manipulations by playing him at his own game. Even though he had bitterly regretted that decision once he had seen just how beautiful Peta Lassiter actually was.

And so he had invited her out on a date just to spite the two schemers, to give them a thrill at the thought that their plan was working. He would leave it up to Peta to choose, he had told himself. If she showed any sign at all of wanting to continue with the relationship he would go along with it. But she had agreed that it was best that they part. Hadn't shown any real interest in seeing him again. Until he had kissed her.

'Yes, I want to know!'

Peta's mouth had set into a stubborn line and her dark eyes met his in defiant challenge. He had to find something to say—and fast!

A day or so ago he might have actually told her the truth. Last night, in the satiated aftermath of their lovemaking, he had almost done so. He had even felt the words forming on his tongue, but had swallowed them down out of sheer bloody cowardice because he had no idea how she felt.

And now he could only thank God that that moment of apprehension had stopped him from spilling his emotional guts out to someone who wouldn't have wanted to hear. That he had caught back the revealing words, I think I'm coming to care for you more than I ever thought possible.

He shuddered inside at the thought that he might have said them. When all the time she had been lying to him, deceiving him deliberately. When she had been taking everything she wanted from this marriage—the house, the wealth—the gifts! Just the thought of the necklace and earrings she had worn with such obvious delight last night made him want to spit.

'Well? Are you going to tell me? Do you have anything to say?'

When had her eyes got so cold? When had she learned to look down her pretty little aristocratic nose at him like that? Or had she always secretly been doing just that? Had he in fact never seen the *real* Peta Farrell until this moment?

Peta *Lassiter*, he corrected himself. Because, at this moment, she was Lassiter through and through. Lassiter blood ran in her veins and Lassiter pride was there in her eyes. The appalling thought that maybe she had known all along what her father was up to in trying to acquire Hewland money to bolster the failing fortunes of the Lassiter family suddenly made his own blood turn to ice in his veins. Maybe she had not only known but willingly gone along with it. The plan might even have been hers all along. She had certainly enjoyed having his money at her disposal.

Perhaps she had decided on a marriage of convenience

right from the start. The sexual attraction between them had just been an unexpected bonus. Something that sweetened the pill she was forced to swallow if she wanted his grandfather's fortune. Something that made the bad bargain of having to be Liam Farrell's wife that little bit easier to bear.

'Anything to say?' he echoed hollowly, eyeing her coldly drawn face with frank distaste. 'Oh, yes, I've plenty to say if you want to hear it.'

'Go ahead.'

Peta forced herself not to back down. If she showed any weakness now he would go for the jugular, attack without mercy, and the only way she could cope with what was to come was to hide behind a careful mask of total indifference. Safer than letting him get anywhere near the truth.

'Why did I marry you?'

He made it sound as if he was actually thinking it through, musing over the question, when she knew that, being Liam, he would already have his answer fully formed and ready. He was just playing with her by pretending to hesitate, drawing out the moment for deliberate effect.

And it was working. Her nerves tightened so much that her bare toes curled tightly on the soft carpet, digging painfully into the thick pile. She jumped, startled and nervous as Liam moved suddenly, but only to stroll over to an armchair set in the bay window. Throwing himself down into it, he stretched out lazily, extending long, powerful legs in front of him and crossing them at the ankles. Leaning his head back against the cushions, he looked up at her through narrowed moss-green eyes.

'You know why.'

'You wanted a child?'

The shrug that lifted the powerful shoulders under the white shirt dismissed the question as irrelevant.

'I never made any secret of it—and neither did you at the time.'

A fact which she couldn't deny. But she thought it better to remain silent and try to ignore the pointed emphasis on that 'at the time'.

'And you were class with a capital C.'

She hadn't expected that, and so she couldn't stop herself from reacting. Her head jerked slightly in shock, her eyes widening. The next moment she had recovered and, following his lead, she moved to sit on the bed, smoothing the ice-blue silk of her robe carefully over her knees. But she *had* reacted, and she knew that Liam had noticed it.

'That was important to you?' Somehow she managed to pitch her voice at a coolly indifferent level, sounding as if the answer to the question didn't matter to her one way or the other.

'It mattered to the old man.'

'Your grandfather?'

His brief brusque inclination of his proud head silently acknowledged that she was right.

'And why did—*class* matter so much to him?'

'He thought it would restore the fallen standing of the Hewland family. That it would go some way towards repairing the damage my irresponsible and reckless mother did to the purity of the bloodline by letting William Farrell father her one child. I might be the black sheep that resulted, but a union with you would restore some much-needed status to the family honour. A child that had you as its mother would help erase the stain on the family crest that resulted in my existence.'

'So that's all I was to you—just a brood mare?'

The taste of misery was bitter on her tongue, eating into her soul like acid, destroying her very being. She had known that he had never loved her, but she had never imagined it would be as bad as this.

He didn't even acknowledge the accusation, let alone try to deny it.

'Not even that, it seems. You don't want my child.'

'I don't want *anyone's* child!'

Not true. Oh, *not* true! She wanted Liam's baby so badly that it was like a permanent ache in her heart. But she didn't dare admit it. Not to him; not even to herself. If she so much as let the thought into her mind she was terrified that he would read it in her face, that he would see the truth in her eyes.

'I couldn't bring a baby into this world—your world.'

'My world!'

His eyes flashed fire, his face dark and dangerous.

'And what do you mean by that?'

'I mean I wouldn't want to—to bring a child into our marriage.'

'You were happy enough to do so at the start.'

'But I wasn't thinking straight. When I did, I realised that I could never have a child in a loveless marriage. A marriage that isn't a real one. I couldn't bring it up in one where—'

'One where I would love it and care for it and give it everything I could? Isn't that what a father's supposed to do?'

'Well, yes. But...'

He would love the child; she knew that. How could she ever doubt that he would care for it? But what about her? Would he ever give her the love she so desperately needed? The love that would make her life complete, fill the empty hole that existed where her heart should be?

'But what?' Liam questioned sharply when she hesitated, the thoughts in her head preventing her from continuing without breaking down. 'What else is there to think about?'

'There's me.'

The look he turned on her was blank, opaque-eyed, emotionless. He seemed to have only just even noticed that she was in the room. That she existed at all. Peta felt as if she wanted to slink away and hide, to bury herself under the bed, crawling in under the valance and disappearing from sight.

'You can have anything you want. You always could.'

'Anything?'

What about your heart? Your love? Your devotion? Your faithfulness for the rest of your life?

She didn't dare to put the thoughts into words and bent her head, staring fixedly at the pattern on the duvet cover so that her dark hair fell forward like a curtain, shielding her revealing face from him.

'Of course. You only have to ask.'

That brought her head up sharply again to glare straight into his coldly set face. Lightning flashes of rejection blazed in the blue depths of her eyes and her soft mouth firmed ominously.

'I don't want to have to *ask!*'

'So you expect me just to know?' Liam flung at her, his voice tight and hard. 'I'm not a bloody mind-reader, woman! I can't tell just by looking at you what you've decided you'd like as a present this time.'

'I'm not talking about presents.'

'Then what *are* you talking about? What do you want? How can I give it to you if you won't say?'

If only she could! She even opened her mouth, reckless enough to finally speak the words, but at the last minute her voice failed her completely and she had to close her lips again, fearful of looking like a gaping fish.

'It wouldn't be enough,' she managed in a strangled voice.

'It was enough for you at the start of this marriage. More than enough.'

'Well, it isn't enough now!'

Liam sighed deeply, raked both hands through the burnished silk of his hair, ruffling it impossibly.

'Okay, what is it going to cost me?'

'What?'

With an effort Peta dragged her attention back to the topic, forcing it away from the sudden rush of need to reach out and smooth the tangle of Liam's hair. Her fingers itched to ease each wayward strand back into place, so much so that she had to clamp them tightly into fists in her lap and hold them there. She knew from experience that if she touched his hair then there would be no going back.

'I said, how much is this going to cost me?'

His words didn't seem to make any sense, and she could only stare at him in blank confusion, blue eyes clouded and unsure.

'Whatever you want. If I can then I'll give it to you. Like I said, you only have to ask.'

'You'd do this—in order to get a child? It means that much to you?'

'Yes.'

It was open and frank, no sign of hesitation, and the jade-green eyes met hers without hesitation, no flicker of embarrassment or doubt showing in them. In fact they were as cold and hard and impenetrable as the stone whose colour they took, smooth and polished as pebbles.

'You think you could *buy* a child?'

That brought a change to his face, a swift flicker of something deep in the unwavering gaze. One moment it was there, the next it was gone, so that she couldn't even be sure that she'd seen it or if in fact she had simply imagined it.

'No. The child would be mine by right. But I know I could buy you. I already have.'

It was too much. The sort of deliberate insult that stabbed straight to her soul like a stiletto. Fine and razor-sharp, the honed blade was capable of inflicting a wound that, while it didn't yet even hurt, would ultimately prove fatal. Shock and despair had numbed the pain he meant to inflict, but Peta knew that deep inside she was bleeding dangerously from the skilfully delivered blow.

'Well, that's where you're wrong.'

The knowledge that she had limited time spurred her on, giving her a sort of fake courage that was meant to cover up how she truly felt. She could only hang on to her composure for a few minutes at most. Then she would collapse, disintegrating into the sort of abject misery that it would humiliate her totally for Liam to see. She had to get rid of him before that. Had to win herself some sort of reprieve, so that she could break her heart in privacy.

'Nothing you can offer me would ever be enough. I don't want anything from you! Nothing at all.'

'Liar.'

It came low and soft, and all the more deadly for being so quiet.

'I know you don't mean a word you say.'

'Oh, but I do!' Peta protested. 'I mean it. And you'd better believe I mean it.'

When he turned one of those cynical, frankly sceptical looks on her again, scouring over her face with the sort of force that seemed to strip away one important defensive layer of skin, she knew that she had to do more. She had to resort to desperate measures if she was ever to have any sort of hope of convincing him.

'Believe me!' she snapped, beyond caring how her

voice sounded, intent only on making him accept her words at any cost. 'And if you won't believe me then believe this…'

In a reckless gesture she lifted her left hand, fingers splayed wide. She pulled at the rings on her third finger. The diamond engagement ring and the gold wedding band that Liam had placed there almost exactly a year before.

It didn't go quite the way she planned. Even the rings seemed to have entered into a conspiracy against her, refusing to move when she tugged. For one appalling moment she thought that she was going to fail to remove them, ruining the gesture completely. But then, just as she was about to despair, the engagement ring came off in her hand, followed swiftly by the wedding band.

'Does this look like a lie? Or this…?'

Thrown with more force than accuracy, the rings landed violently, one on Liam's shoulder, the other on the exposed skin of his chest. A moment later they bounced off again, to land on the carpet with soft thuds.

'I don't want to wear your rings any more. I don't want to be your wife and I *don't* want to have your children.'

The worst, the most appalling thing about Liam's reaction, was his total lack of it. Throughout the little drama that she had just performed in front of him he had sat there, completely motionless, scarcely blinking, barely even seeming to breathe. He had simply regarded her with a coolly dispassionate scrutiny, no trace of any response or emotion showing in the cold, set lines of his face. He might have been carved from marble for all that he revealed about his thoughts, his feelings. And Peta, struggling with her breathing and the way her throat seemed to have closed up tightly, felt as if she was some sort of clinically dissected specimen on a laboratory slab, being studied with total indifference and a complete lack of emotion.

Say something! she willed him inwardly, knowing she couldn't bear the silence tugging cruelly at her nerves to drag out any longer. But when Liam finally drew breath to speak she knew that she was afraid of what he might say. Then she didn't know which would be worse in the end.

'No children?' he said at last, his voice as expressionless as his face.

'No children.'

Surprisingly it had more conviction than she had thought she could manage. Somehow the fact that she had to hold her lips taut and stiff in order to stop them from quivering in a weakness she didn't want him to see meant that her words could come out with an icy brittleness that she had never quite planned.

'I married you for children.' His control was complete, terrifyingly so.

'Then tough. I refuse to be a brood mare for you and your grandfather.'

At last he showed something, but if it was an emotion then she couldn't interpret what it was. His eyes narrowed briefly, calculatingly, and his mouth closed tight, as if cutting off the words he had planned to say, only to think better of it almost at once.

'That's your decision,' he said flatly.

'Yes, it's my decision! And it's one I don't…'

Her voice failed her, the words shrivelling on her tongue as he pushed himself suddenly to his feet, his imposing height and the width of his powerful chest and shoulders awe-inspiring enough to drive all coherent thought from her mind.

'I…' she tried again, but Liam totally ignored her.

'I thought you understood the terms of our agreement,' he told her, every word seeming to be formed in blocks of ice. 'No child, no marriage. You can't have one without the other.'

'And if I don't want either?'

*What was she saying?* She didn't seem to have any control over her tongue any more. She didn't think the words; nothing formed in her brain. She just opened her mouth and heard the dreadful, appalling, ruinously destructive phrases come out, flowing without hesitation where before she had never even had the nerve to consider them. Even if she was trying to get him to go, so that she could have a little time to herself, to try and lick her wounds in peace, then did she have to go quite this far?

'No child, no marriage,' Liam came back at her again. 'No marriage, no cash. It's as simple as that.'

Peta's mind reeled in horror. Did he truly think that she was so shallow that she would actually consider rethinking her declaration because of the money?

Oh, why was she even asking herself? Of course he thought it! Why else would he have said it? She had to refute the implied accusation, but her tongue seemed to have turned to wood in her mouth, refusing to form a single word.

'Tough choice, sweetheart? So what happened to that "it's not enough"?'

To her amazement he was actually *smiling*. It wasn't a warm smile. In fact it was the most fiendish, hateful smile she had ever seen, and it froze the blood in her veins.

'You see, you didn't get all the facts when you married me, darling,' he drawled lazily, the cynical emphasis on the last word taking it to a point that was light years away from any term of affection. 'You may have seen this marriage as the way into the Hewland estate and all that goes with it, but my grandfather put one or two conditions into his will. If I don't provide him with a legitimate heir while he's still alive then the whole of the estate goes to a home for retired racehorses.'

'But…'

Peta couldn't believe what she was hearing. She knew that Joshua Hewland was a difficult and a narrow-minded old man, but she had never believed that he would go quite this far. What man would cut his own grandson out of his will just for spite?

'You can't mean it! I don't believe you!'

'Believe it! Like I said—no child, no cash. It's as simple as that. And divorce isn't an option—it just ensures that the racehorses get the estate. Face it, lady. I had to. There's no way out.'

He was turning as he spoke, heading for the door. The two rings she had flung at him still lay on the floor, in his path. With a swift, disdainful movement of one foot, he kicked them out of his way, driving them both under the bed, where they disappeared from view. The gesture was so expressive of the way he felt about her and their marriage that Peta felt as if cruel hands were wrenching her heart in two.

'Where are you going?'

She didn't know why she asked, only that she couldn't just let him go without doing it. Deep inside she was suddenly very afraid that he would walk out of her life, disappear for good, without even a backward glance.

'Out.'

It was tossed over his shoulder at her, Liam not even pausing on his way out of the room.

'I have to get out of this house—get some fresh air into my lungs. Quite frankly, I find the stench of greed and deceit in here totally oppressive.'

But then, unexpectedly, he turned in the doorway, subjecting her to a savagely contemptuous survey, eyes flicking over her from the top of her dark head to where her bare feet rested on the carpet.

'If you're wise, you'll take the time while I'm away to think things through. Decide what you want and what you're prepared to do to get it.'

'I told you…' Peta began, but he cut off her attempt at speech with an arrogant wave of one strong hand.

'Yes, I know what you told me—but that was before I told *you* that there was nothing to be gained from leaving me and everything to be won by staying. If you want the money, sweetheart—any money at all—then you have to stick with this marriage. It's as simple as that. Think about it, darling. I'm sure you'll soon see sense.'

'I'd rather starve!'

Even Peta didn't know whether she meant it or not. Right now she had no idea whether what she felt for Liam was total blind foolish love or equally wholehearted hatred. Either way, it seemed that nothing she did could touch him.

'That could be arranged,' he returned with cold-blooded nonchalance, twisting on his heel once more and heading for the stairs. 'If that's what you want—then go for the divorce option. Half of nothing is still nothing.'

It was only as the door swung to behind him and she heard the sound of his footsteps descending the staircase and crossing the hall that Peta felt she really understood the true meaning of loneliness. Without Liam there, even an angry, bitter, and harsh-voiced Liam, the room seemed so empty and cold. And she felt totally alone. Completely lost.

'Liam…' she tried to call after him. 'Liam—please don't go. Please stay and talk—and maybe we can sort this out. Please—please—come back…'

Her voice broke, finally failed her, and then the heavy,

oppressive, total silence was the only thing she could hear. Even Liam's footsteps had died away into the distance.

And she had no way of knowing whether he really hadn't heard her attempt to call him back. Or whether, far worse, he *had* heard, but had deliberately ignored her, hardening his heart even further as he walked away.

# CHAPTER EIGHT

WHAT the hell was he doing? Liam asked himself as he strode across the landing and down the stairs.

Just what had possessed him to make up that pack of lies and throw it at Peta?

Okay, so *all* of it wasn't a lie. His grandfather *was* a narrow-minded old bigot who was perfectly capable of carrying out his threat to hand the Hewland estate over to the home for retired racehorses just to spite everyone—himself included. But even if that happened then it still wouldn't leave his grandson on the poverty line. Or anywhere near it.

One of the few good things that he had inherited from his father had been William Farrell's ability to deal with numbers and an instinct for guessing at odds. Luckily, Liam had put that ability to use on the stock market, not on the racetrack that had so often tempted his father, and the resulting fortune he had made for himself would keep both him and his wife in comfort for the rest of their lives.

Okay, so it didn't have the prestige and the lineage as long as your arm that mattered so much to old Joshua and the Lassiters—and apparently to Peta too, he told himself, as he reached the tiled hallway and headed for the cloakroom, but it was more than enough.

So why had he pretended that he would be left close to penniless if he didn't inherit his grandfather's estate? he was forced to wonder as he pulled on a thick windproof jacket, all the time scowling darkly at an ornately decorated Christmas tree that stood, lights still burning brightly, at the foot of the stairs.

Some Christmas this was going to turn out to be! Last year at this time he had hoped that he was actually on the road towards having something he'd dreamed of ever since he was a boy. A home of his own, a family—or, at the very least, the hope of a family on the way. He had truly believed that Peta wanted children as much as he did. It had never crossed his mind that she might be lying through her white little teeth in order to get her hands on the fortune to which she thought she was entitled.

He hated her for that! Hated her for the deception she had practised, for the pretence that she shared something of the same dreams as he did. But most of all he detested the greed that she had shown.

He had actually thought that she was different. That she wasn't like her parents or his grandfather. But her greed had dropped her right into his hands, so that now he could play the puppet master and pull her strings whichever way he wanted.

'But *why?*'

The question escaped into the cold morning air as he stood, his fingers stilling on the buttons of his coat, to consider the situation that he had landed himself in.

'Why should I even want to do that?'

Why would he do anything at all that would stop his lying, conniving, greedy wife walking out, as she had wanted? Why would he do or say something that would make her reconsider her threat to leave him, to end this marriage before it had truly begun?

Because he wanted her to stay.

'Oh, *hell!*' he groaned out loud, shaking his head in despair at his own folly. 'Oh damn, damn, damn it to hell! I've really got this bad.'

It was far worse than he had thought. He had proposed marriage to Peta on an impulse, not thinking things through, because he hadn't been able to bear the thought of letting her go. He had never felt an incandescent heat of passion like that for any woman before. And, although it wasn't the traditional hearts and flowers and happy-ever-after that sentiment would have you believe was vital for a successful marriage, he had been sure that between them they could make things work. They shared enough, didn't they? The desire for each other for one thing—the longing for children for another.

Except that Peta hadn't wanted children, damn her!

But he had wanted *Peta*, and that had blinded him, switching off his intelligence and replacing it with another, far more basic way of thinking.

And he still wanted her. More than was sensible. More than any sane man should want any woman. Fool that he was—blind, stupid, bloody fool—he didn't want to let her go. And that was why he had made up the story about the poor return for her investment if she divorced him now.

A faint sound behind the big oak-wood door brought his head swinging round, but a moment later the silence had returned, making him think he had imagined it. Either that or it had been just a bird or some other small creature outside.

He had to get out, he told himself. Had to get out into the air and clear his thoughts. He didn't know whether he was coming or going. One moment he detested Peta, ab-horring everything she stood for. The next he knew that he just couldn't tolerate the thought of a future without her in it. Was he really going to be fool enough to try to persuade her to stay—by whatever means?

'No!'

Furious with himself for his weakness, he swung round sharply, planning on going back upstairs.

He would tell her to go. To get out of his life and never come back. He was well rid of her. Never wanted to see her lovely—her *lying* face again!

Oh, but he did!

Even as his foot touched the first tread of the stairs he froze again, knowing he couldn't do it.

If he went upstairs now—walked into that room, saw her standing there, tall, slender and elegant, long dark hair tumbled around that beautiful face, the ice-blue silk of her robe clinging in all the right places...

Oh, God help him! If he went in there now, he was far more likely to grab hold of her, kiss her senseless—as senseless as he felt right at this moment—and tumble her onto the bed...

Already his body was hard as rock just to *think* of it, just to imagine her soft, perfumed flesh underneath him, her mouth opening to him, her body yielding... So what would he do if he had to contend with the reality?

Face it, he told himself resignedly. Face the facts— she's got her hooks into you good and proper, and you'll never get her out of your system unless...

Unless...

Slowly Liam brought his foot back down onto the hall tiles, leaning against the wall and folding his arms across his chest as he made himself think through the idea that had just slid into his head. Perhaps there *was* a way of handling this so that he could have his cake and eat it. A way to make sure that his grasping little wife got what she wanted—and so did he.

The more he considered it, the more he realised that it could work. He could have Peta right where he wanted her, for as long as he wanted her—and then, when he'd got what he wanted out of this—but only then—he would give her the pay-off she'd been dreaming of.

But first he'd let her stew for a bit. What was it they said? That revenge was a dish best eaten cold? Well, he'd leave her to cool down some, take that walk he needed, and then he'd put the proposition to her. Maybe when she'd had time to sit and contemplate the future with the prospect of a nil return on her investment she'd be more than happy to accept the compromise he offered.

She'd probably snatch his hand off, he told himself, smiling grimly as he pulled back the big bolts on the door, wrenched it open.

It had started to snow, he realised. Just a faint, light powdering that had sprinkled the driveway and the wide lawns beyond the glass doors and huge windows of the porch that framed the entrance. But the heavy grey clouds, the leaden colour of the sky, promised more to come—and plenty of it.

A white Christmas, he thought, reflecting cynically that images of snow-covered fields and hills were all very well on Christmas cards. In reality they were a nuisance and brought endless problems just getting through the day. But the weather suited his mood, cold and grim and hard as ice.

He was folding up his collar around his neck, fastening the very top button against the bitter cold, when he heard the noise again.

A faint, soft, snuffling sort of sound, like a breath being drawn in and then let go, easing out on a sigh. A noise like nothing he'd ever heard here or in Hewland woods before. And it didn't resemble the sound of any form of wildlife he recognised either.

'What…?'

It was as he moved forward that he saw it. And the sight was so totally unexpected, so completely bemusing, that he came to a complete stop and just stood and stared, unable to believe that he could actually be seeing straight.

'How did *you* get here?'

Peta had finally accepted that Liam was not coming back, At least, not in the immediate future. But then she had never really expected that he would. After the dreadful words she had flung at him, the way he had walked out, she didn't really expect to see him again before night-fall—if then. But still she had made herself stay where she was, perched on the edge of the bed, listening, and waiting.

But there was no point in waiting any longer. For one thing she knew she had angered and alienated him so much that it would be all he could do to ever speak to her again, and for another, more practical reason, she couldn't sit around in this flimsy silky robe any longer. The small glimpse of the garden she could see through a crack in the curtains warned that today was going to be a typical late-December day. Cold and miserable, with a lowering grey sky and the promise of snow, if she wasn't mistaken.

A white Christmas, she told herself as she stood under the shower with the water pounding down on her head. As a child she had loved the snow, running outside in it as soon as she possibly could, making snowmen, building igloos, and swooshing down the long steep hill near her home on the ancient toboggan that had once been her father's.

But there would be none of that this year. No one to share the delights of playing in the snow or sledging down a hill. After the nasty scene between her and Liam this morning she would be lucky if she had a husband to spend Christmas with, she thought miserably, switching off the shower and hurrying out to snatch up a towel. Even after long minutes spent under the hot cascade of water she still felt cold and shivery. An inner coldness, a misery of the soul that no physical comfort could reach. And one that was likely to remain with her for a very long time. Maybe even for the rest of her life.

Certainly, she only felt a very little better when she had

dried herself and pulled on jeans and a warm lavender cashmere sweater, brushing her dark hair viciously until it was absolutely straight and then confining it in a covered elastic band so that it was held severely back from her face. There was no point in any make-up—no one was here to see her—so she simply rubbed a slick of moisturiser over her skin and then turned to make a face at herself in the dressing table mirror.

'Death warmed up,' she muttered ruefully. 'Not so warmed, if it comes to that! You look awful!'

A trace of female pride made her reach for the mascara and sweep a single coat of it over the length of her lashes, seeing that at least it opened up her heavy eyes just a little. But the shadows underneath them were another matter, as were the drawn lines around her nose and mouth. She would need special make-up work to disguise them. The sort of careful attention to detail that was quite frankly beyond her right now.

'It'll have to do,' she told her reflection with a grimace. 'After all, it's not as if anyone's going to be here.'

No one but Liam, she added mentally, seeing the thought register as a cloud in the dark blue of her eyes, flattening out any curve to her mouth. And the mood Liam would be in, she'd be surprised if he even *looked* at her, let alone noticed anything about her appearance.

'Peta!'

The call came from downstairs, startling her into dropping the mascara wand, because it was the last thing she was expecting. The last thing she believed she would hear. So she had to be imagining things, she told herself. A bad case of wish fulfilment—or, rather, dreaming of wish fulfilment. Liam must be miles away by now.

But she hadn't heard the door slam. Or the sound of his car engine revving up outside.

'*Peta!* Are you there?'

There was no mistaking it this time. Definitely her name. And definitely Liam calling her.

*Liam calling her!*

Wonderful phrases like change of mind, second thoughts, whole new perspective, rushed into her head, making her whirl and dash frantically for the door. If he was prepared to forgive and forget, maybe even kiss and make up, then she wasn't going to put any barriers in his way. If anything she would be there before him, only too ready and willing to offer the olive branch.

*'Peta!'*

'I'm coming!'

There was an ominous note in the repetition of her name, but she didn't let it trouble her. Liam had never been the most patient of men. And surely the edginess indicated that he didn't want to hang about—that he wanted to start peace talks just as soon as possible.

Out on the landing, she leaned over the polished wooden banisters, peering down into the hall. Even at this precarious angle she still couldn't quite see him, except as a bulky shadow between herself and the limited light from the window.

'What is it? What do you wa…?'

'Get down here! *Now!* I need you!'

That 'Get down here…' wasn't exactly cajoling, but the impatience in the 'Now' and the 'I need you' more than made up for it.

'Okay, I'm coming!'

Not caring that it might not be the most sensible thing in the world to let him see just how much effect he could have on her, how easily she would respond to him, and totally ignoring the furious cries of her outraged sense of self-preservation, Peta flew down the stairs, clattering and stumbling in her haste to obey.

She leaped the last three steps in one, landing lightly

on the tiled floor and swaying for a moment as she re-
gained her balance. Only then did she turn to face Liam,
her heart racing, her eyes wide and bright, her cheeks
faintly flushed.

'I'm here! What is it? What do you…?'

He didn't look as pleased to see her as she had anticipated. Instead, his face was set into strangely grim lines,
his dark brows drawn together in a frown. His green eyes
had a disturbingly opaque cast to them, one that made
them look faintly distant and—annoyed? No—concerned—that was the right word.

And then he moved and she saw what he held and her
heart jolted just once, sharply, painfully, all the breath
escaping from her lungs in a rushed exclamation of disbelief.

'Liam! Just what is that!'

He was holding something in his arms. A parcel. A
large, rectangular box covered in bright wrapping paper,
decorated with robins and dancing snowmen.

A gift? No, instinctively she knew that just wasn't
likely. The mood that Liam had been in when he walked
out of the bedroom it had to be more than unlikely that
he would have even thought of giving her a present—
unless it could have been divorce papers tied with a gold
ribbon. And besides, she suspected that dancing snowmen
weren't quite his thing. Then there was the fact that the
wrapping paper looked to be of the cheapest, most mass-
produced kind—again two things that she didn't readily
associate with Liam, who liked quality and style in everything.

The lid of the box was open, and through the top she
could just see something white and quilted, though she
couldn't quite make out what. Even as she was wondering
something in the parcel made a small snuffling sound.

And then, totally unexpectedly, the white quilted fabric gave a sudden, jerking movement.

'Liam…?'

'Here—take this…'

He pushed the parcel at her, forcing her to hold out her hands automatically and take it solely in order to stop it from falling onto the floor.

'What…?'

But words failed her completely as she looked down at the 'parcel' and saw at one end of the box, partially muffled in the fabric, which turned out to be something like a miniature sleeping bag, the pink, angelic face of a sleeping baby.

'*Liam!* Liam, this is a *baby!*'

'Yes.' His attention was obviously elsewhere. 'Look after her for me.'

'Look… But where did it—she?—come from? Where are you going?'

He was turning away, heading for the door, and obviously didn't intend to answer her.

'Liam…'

Awkwardly she managed to reach out one-handedly and catch hold of the sleeve of his jacket, struggling to balance the box and its precious contents at the same time.

'What is happening? Where—?'

'I have to go and try to find her mother…'

His eyes were dark and strangely unfocused, his attention clearly miles away from here—and from her, his thoughts on something else.

'She might still be around.'

'Liam, please. You're not making sense. Where did this baby come from? Where's her mother?'

'I don't damn well know!' he exploded, making the baby stir restively. 'I just found her here—on the porch,' he went on, adjusting the volume down a level or two, but for the baby's sake only.

All too obviously his antagonism towards Peta herself had not lessened. If anything the bleakness of his expression, the green shards of ice that were his eyes, revealed that his mood was even worse than when he had walked out on her a short time before.

'So, whoever put her there must still be somewhere around.'

'Out there?'

Peta glanced towards the drive, where the snow that had threatened was already starting to fall—heavy white flakes drifting slowly down to the frozen earth where it was clear that they were going to settle.

'But, Liam, the weather's—'

'Do you think I don't know that?' he cut in on her savagely. 'That's precisely why I have to go and search for her. Are you going to look after the baby or not?'

'Do I have any choice?'

It sounded far more ungracious than she had meant.

'I'm sorry. Of course you have to go and look for the mother. I'll cope here.'

For a brief moment the bleakness of his eyes lightened. There was even a touch of warmth, or at the very least gratitude in the swift glance he flashed her, and the grim set of his mouth almost softened—though not quite into a smile.

'Thanks.'

It was raw and grating, as if it came from a painfully sore throat.

'I'll be back as soon as I can. There's some stuff for her in there. Bottles, feed…that sort of thing…'

A wave of his hand indicated a supermarket plastic carrier bag that stood on the floor, leaning against the wall, its bulky shape indicating that several things had been pushed in, haphazard and probably in a rush.

'I'll manage.'

She hoped she sounded more confident than she actually felt. It wasn't just the thought of looking after the baby that concerned her. There was something else going on here. Something she didn't understand and couldn't quite get a grasp on. She felt as if she was struggling with dark dangerous currents, swirling round the jagged edges of rocks that could cause terrible damage at any moment. And the worst thing about the feeling was that she had no idea why.

'Oh—'

Liam was almost out through the door, but he paused for a moment on the doorstep, letting the icy wind and the wildly whirling snowflakes into the warm hallway.

'Her name's Alice. I'll be back as soon as I can.'

And he was gone before she could say anything. Before she could ask the obvious question.

'So how does he know that you're Alice?' Peta mused wonderingly, addressing the question to the sleeping baby. 'Does he know who you are?'

Of course there was no answer, and, smiling faintly at her own foolishness in even asking the question out loud, she reached out a foot and kicked the door firmly closed.

'It's cold in here! No place for a little person like you— let's get you into the warmth.'

The sitting room was dark and shadowed, the heavy brocade curtains still drawn closed from the previous night, shutting out the light. But it was more than that, Peta told herself, hurrying to put the baby and her gaudily wrapped box carefully on the settee before yanking the curtains open with rough, jerky movements. The echoes of last night still lingered, memories of the passion that had swept over them seeming to hang in the air like the scent of incense, making her feel edgy and uncomfortable.

But what are you feeling uncomfortable about? she asked herself, catching sight of her reflection in the big wall mirror and addressing her question towards it. You knew all along that Liam didn't love you. That he only married you because he wanted a child so badly. So why should it matter so much more to have him say it?

Because it did matter. And it hurt. It hurt far more than she had ever anticipated. She felt as if her heart was raw and bleeding from a wound that would never heal.

Because deep down inside what she was really struggling to face was the thought that her one foolish, personal dream could never, ever come true. With those coldly enunciated words he had tossed at her upstairs Liam had not just confirmed the past, he had taken away the hope of a future. He had destroyed totally the possibility that one day he might come to love her, and see her as more than just a babymaking and carrying machine.

'So it looks like you're going to be the only baby I ever get to take care of—at least here, in this house, sweetie,' she told the sleeping Alice, bending down over the make-shift crib to stroke the infant's velvet-soft cheek. 'Unless I agree to have Liam's child and put up with knowing that he doesn't love me.'

The image that sprang into her mind was just too painful to bear, bringing with it the hot sting of tears, and the cruel bite of despair.

How could she face such a future? How could she stand to conceive, to carry, to give birth to Liam's baby and then watch it grow, knowing that her baby's father would never love her? How could she stay always on the side-lines, knowing that Liam loved his son or daughter—because he would love his child, she had no doubt about that—and yet accepting the fact that he felt nothing for the woman who had given it to him?

And when that child was older, when, inevitably, as it matured, it started to ask questions, how would she be able to answer them? How could she look her son or daughter in the face when they demanded to know where babies came from and tell them something that just wasn't true? She would never be able to say, as her mother had said to her, that 'when two people love each other very much they do something very special.'

'Oh, Alice!'

This time she couldn't hold back the tears, because she remembered the rest of the words her mother had used to explain things.

'Some people call it sex, Peta,' she had said. 'But when it's right—when it's special—then it's called making love.'

And now, years later, those words came back to haunt her, wrenching her soul in pain at the thought that while she had been truly making love with Liam, he had only ever been having sex with her.

'Oh, Alice, sweetie!' she moaned, tears flooding down her cheeks. 'Whatever am I going to do?'

And perhaps because she heard her name, or simply because the noise of Peta's sobs disturbed her slumber, the baby stirred, opened wide blue eyes, blinked, whimpered, and then, as if registering that she was in completely strange surroundings, finally let rip with a full-scale roar of distress that made it plain she wanted attention—and she wanted it *now!*

# CHAPTER NINE

IT WAS the middle of the afternoon by the time Liam returned home.

Because the shortest day of the year had only just passed, the early signs of dusk were already gathering to darken the sky and dim what little light had penetrated the thick clouds during the afternoon. The snow that those clouds had carried had already fallen, eased, and then come back again, in full force this time, so that the faint sprinkling of white over the lawns and drive had turned into a thin blanket, covering everything. And now more was falling, adding inches to that first fine layer.

He sighed and pulled off his coat, tossing it in the general direction of a hook as he stamped his feet hard to rid them of the clinging flakes of snow. The action also expressed his feelings.

He was cold, he was hungry, but most of all he was in a thoroughly bad mood. His hunt for the baby's mother had proved totally unrewarding and a sense of impotent frustration burned like acid in the pit of his stomach.

Where the hell could Lucy have got to? He had looked everywhere he could think she might be. Or was there somewhere else he could have tried?

His thoughts were still fretting away at the subject when he opened the door to the sitting room. The sight that met his eyes there drove away everything else from his head.

Peta was sitting on the big gold-coloured settee, her legs curled up under her so that she looked like a small girl, cuddling down contentedly. She was holding the tiny, white-clothed bundle that was the baby Alice, the little

117

girl's down-covered head resting safely in the crook of one of her arms. The other hand held a bottle of milk at which the infant was sucking greedily, small, grunting noises of contentment escaping her as she fed. The lights in the big room weren't switched on, but at some point in the day Peta had lit a fire and the brightly flickering flames spread a warm glow across the face that was watching the child so intently.

It was a sight that took his breath away, administering a hard, yearning kick that had him muffling the groan he couldn't hold back. The thought that right there before him was all he wanted—all he had ever wanted—took root in his thoughts and wouldn't go away. He wanted nothing more than to stay exactly where he was. To simply stand in silence and watch.

But then that hastily suppressed groan, or some other sound he hadn't been aware of making, caught Peta's attention, bringing her dark head up in a rush, her blue eyes coming swiftly to his watchful face.

'Oh, there you are! At last! I thought you were never coming home!'

Something in her words, in the tone of her voice, flicked him on the raw, aggravating an already crabby mood.

'I've been looking for Alice's mother. I didn't want to come back until I found her!'

'And did you? You managed it? Where is she?'

'I have no damn idea! None at all. Do you think that I would have come back if I could have thought of anywhere else to look?'

'You didn't find her?'

She sounded thoroughly disappointed. But not as disappointed as he felt.

'Do I look as though I did?' he snarled, turning in a

brusque movement to snap on the main lights, bringing the whole room into sharply defined, brilliant clarity.

And when he turned back it was as if the spotlight of reality had been shone onto the scene before him, destroying the delusion of just moments before.

Because it had been a delusion, not the truth. Just the fantasy of what he hoped for superimposing itself on top of the actuality that in fact existed. He had seen what he wanted to see. Not what really *was*.

'Can you see any sign of anyone else with me?'

'I just thought… I hoped…'

He knew what she'd hoped for; the dissatisfaction in her tone told him that with no room for the comfort of self-deception. She had hoped that he would bring Alice's mother back here tonight so that she could hand the little girl over to her parent and be done with it. She was annoyed and discontented to find that she couldn't do just that.

'Well, I'm sorry to disappoint you but I didn't find her. Not even anyone who'd seen her or knew where she was.'

The maternal image that had presented itself to his eyes as he opened the door evaporated in a couple of bitterly depressing seconds. He knew where it had come from and the realisation only added to his already cruel sense of being badly let down.

He'd overdosed on Christmas and everything that went with it, on the image of mother and child that was on almost every second one of the cards already displayed around the room, pictures imbued with a tenderness of love and devotion that was normally at the core of that special relationship.

And right outside the village church was a large traditional Christmas crib. He'd walked past it several times today on his frustrating quest to find someone who might know where Lucy could have hidden herself. The figures in the roughly crafted little stable were half life-size, vividly realistic, and the Madonna figure there had just the loving expression on her face that he had foolishly let himself imagine had been on Peta's when he opened the door.

Peta and the Madonna, that was a laugh! He'd had some stupid illusions about his wife in the past, but that had to be one of the best! Just who was he trying to kid?

And only now did he realise what had sparked the rush of annoyance as soon as he had arrived. In the first moment Peta had spoken she had sounded so edgy and unwelcoming. 'I thought you were never coming home,' she'd said. *Home.* But never before had the house ever seemed quite so unlike his own home as it had in that moment.

'I've drawn a total blank!'

'That's a pity. So what do we do now?'

In Peta's arms the baby drained the last of her milk and released the bottle teat with a loud spluttering sound. Immediately Peta's eyes dropped to consider the small scrap of humanity she held.

'All gone! Well done! This little girl has an amazing appetite! That's the second time I've had to feed her since you left, and it's nothing like four hours since the last bottle. Come on, then, Alice—any wind to get rid of?'

Gently she hoisted the baby into a sitting position, holding her upright carefully and rubbing the flat of one hand over her back. Alice's head was already lolling sleepily, her eyes drooping as she blew a small, milky bubble from her soft pink mouth. The bubble was followed seconds later by a loud, unladylike belch that echoed through the sudden hush in the room.

'Good girl!'

She glanced swiftly up at him, amusement lighting her

eyes. Amusement that died as swiftly as it had come, to
be replaced by a return to her earlier edginess.

'I'd better just get her cleaned up and then she'll probably sleep again. If you could just pass me the bag. There
are nappies in there…'

She was talking to dispel the silence, Peta admitted.
Chattering inanely, saying anything simply so that she
didn't have to wonder just what Liam was thinking. She
didn't know what was going on behind those deep, dark
green eyes of his, what thoughts were filling his mind.
She only knew that in the moment that he had switched
on the light and she had seen his face her spirits had
plunged right down, hitting rock-bottom almost at once.

If he had been in a difficult and unpredictable mood
when he had set out to look for Alice's mother then he
had returned in an even worse one now. The feeling that
there were dark undercurrents she didn't understand was
back again, even more unsettling than before. He wouldn't
even look at her as he snatched up the plastic carrier bag.

'Shall I do it?'

'Do you know how to change a nappy?'

At his slightly shamefaced look a tiny flutter of laughter
escaped, dying at once as soon as it encountered the darkness in his eyes.

'I'll do it this time. You've been out all day. Did you
go far?'

'All round the village—and out to Holton.'

'You must have walked for miles. In this weather!'

'It wasn't too bad to start with. The snow only really
started to come down in the last hour or so.'

It was only when she came closer to collect the bag of
nappies that Peta realised that what she had thought were
shadows cast by the gathering dusk on his face were in
fact marks of weariness. And when his hands were free
he lifted them, rubbing his palms on his eyes, before rak-

ing his fingers through the short crisp strands of his hair. Something twisted sharply deep in her heart. A sudden tug of sympathy for the way that he was obviously tired and disappointed at his lack of success.

'You look worn out. Have you eaten anything at all?'

He didn't answer, but his face gave everything away all the same.

'Just give me a minute and I'll find something for you. I need to put Alice down to sleep first.'

'Put her where?'

Liam's clouded gaze went to where the cardboard box that the baby had arrived in lay discarded by the side of the fire. Empty now, it looked the worse for wear, drab and shabby, the tears in the paper showing clearly where they had been mended with sticky tape.

'Not there.' Peta had followed the direction of his glance.

She indicated where the top drawer from a chest upstairs stood on the table.

'Very inventive of you.' Liam's tone was impossible to interpret.

'Not really. I remembered once I'd read somewhere that for a little baby an empty drawer made a safe enough cot, so I improvised. A couple of blankets for padding, and her little quilted sleeping bag, and she's as snug as can be.'

She hadn't expected praise. A simple word of thanks would have done. She would even have settled for just an acknowledgement. What she didn't anticipate was the way that his expression remained blank as stone, his eyes showing no response. If she had been talking about the price of fish at the supermarket he couldn't have been less interested.

And what did you expect, idiot? she upbraided herself. The Nobel Prize for baby care? This is *Liam* you're talking to. The guy who made it plain that all he wanted from you was your breeding—'Class with a capital C'. He's not worried about whether you can look after a child or even love it. Only that it has your genes, your bloodline and his mixed in its veins.

Unnerved by the stinging threat of tears, the tears she had thought she had cried out earlier this morning, she knew she had to get out of the room fast before she gave herself away.

'I'll take her to the bathroom to change her,' she said sharply, imposing a vicious effort of will to ensure that her weakness didn't show in her voice. 'It's easier that way. You sit down and get warm and I'll get you something to eat just as soon as I'm done.'

'I can make a sandwich myself. You don't need to worry about it.'

Liam's comment caught her painfully on the raw, making her mood swing once more from one extreme to another. This time the reassuring flare of anger at what she saw as an implied insult was more than welcome, driving away just a little of the earlier misery and putting something more protective in its place.

'I can manage a sandwich and soup at least! I'm not going to poison you with that!'

To her consternation she saw the firm, fine lines of his mouth twitch in something that looked suspiciously like amusement. But it was only there for a second and then it was gone.

'I do have experience of your cooking, remember,' he murmured drily.

Peta had to concede the justification of the comment. Cooking was not her forte. Somehow the skills that made her mother such a wonderful meal-maker had totally passed her by. The few dishes she had tried to prepare in the early days of their marriage had been either burnt offerings, almost totally cremated, or at the opposite extreme, coming very close to being raw. She had improved a bit since then, but most of the time she left the cooking to the housekeeper.

'Mrs Dillon made the soup. And even I can't spoil buttering a couple of slices of bread and putting some cheese between them.'

'Okay, then. I'll risk it.'

The ease with which he gave in, when normally he would argue, stubborn as a terrier, over the slightest thing, gave Peta a disturbing indication of just how low he was feeling. Tiredness? Or something else? She couldn't get beneath the emotionless surface of the careful mask that was all he would show her in order to find out.

'I'll be back in a minute.'

His only response was a faint nod of his dark head. His whole attention was on the baby who had now fallen asleep in her arms. And as Peta watched he reached out a hand and touched the little girl's face, just one long finger resting lightly against the tiny cheek.

The contrast between the width and power of his hand and the delicacy of the baby's fine bone structure caught on the vulnerable, wounded part of Peta's heart, making the tears burn again so that she had to blink violently in order to force them back.

'Better get Pudding here cleaned up!' she said, with an unnatural loudness that was the perverse result of trying to control her voice. 'I won't be long.'

And, grateful for the chance to escape from the emotionally fraught atmosphere of the room, she fled out into the hall and up the stairs.

She took her time changing and cleaning the baby, only going back downstairs when she thought she could handle facing Liam again. She wasn't actually *ready* to be with him, but she suspected that if she waited any longer he would come after her, wanting to know what had kept her.

And so she splashed cold water on her face to cool her burning eyes, drew a long, deep breath and made herself walk calmly down into the sitting room again.

He was on the settee, sitting with his elbows on his knees, his chin resting in the palms of his hands, staring into the fire as if he could read some mystical message in the shapes formed by the dancing flames. He barely glanced up as she settled Alice in the makeshift drawer bed, only stirring some minutes later when, having been to the kitchen, she returned with a bowl of soup and a plateful of sandwiches and placed them on the coffee-table beside him.

'Thanks.' It was abstracted, his mind clearly on other things.

Well, Peta had her own things to worry about.

'Liam, about Alice,' she said as she settled in the chair to the right of the fire. 'Liam?'

It obviously took him a moment to pull himself out of whatever had absorbed him, shaking his head faintly as if to clear his thoughts as he turned to face her.

'What about Alice?'

'Isn't it obvious? What are we going to do with her? I mean we can't keep her. Don't you think we should tell Social Services or someone? Someone official.'

That got through to him. At last he seemed to come alive, rejection of her suggestion sparking in the mossy depths of his eyes.

'No way.'

'But, Liam—we have to—'

'I said no way!'

The ferocity in his voice startled her, making her flinch back in her seat.

'I'm sorry.'

Seeing her reaction, Liam hastily adjusted his tone downwards, with an obvious effort.

'We can't hand her over to Social Services. Once they're involved—'

'But they have to be involved! That's what they're there for—for cases like this. It's their job.'

'No.'

Low and quiet, it still had far more force than his earlier, more emphatic response, and it kept her silent when she knew she should protest some more.

'Let me explain,' Liam said, after a pause that stretched her nerves taut as violin strings, wondering what was coming next. 'It's rather more complicated than just any abandoned baby.'

'Complicated how?'

'I know who Alice's mother is.'

She hadn't expected that, and it shocked her rigid, making her sit up sharply and stare at him.

'You…? How?'

'She lives in the village. I know her well. She's always been a little wild—a little out of control.'

'And how do you know that this—this…'

'Her name's Lucy,' Liam supplied, knowing what she was looking for.

'That this Lucy is Alice's mother? And how do you know she's called Alice, come to that?'

'There was a note in the box with her. It said that her name was Alice—and a couple of other things.'

'And this "couple of other things"—they told you that Alice's mother was this Lucy?'

A slow, thoughtful nod was his only response.

'Can I see this note?'

She knew his response before he gave it. His instant recoil was obvious, the fact that he didn't want her to see it only too clear.

'I don't have it on me. I must have left it somewhere. But I know that Lucy is Alice's mother. And because of that I also know that if we get Social Services involved then Lucy could get into a real mess.'

'And she's not in one now? What sort of mother…?'

'I know! And that's my whole point. Lucy already had some problems before this. Mixing with the wrong sort of kids. A couple of brushes with the law. Nothing too serious, but enough to give her a record. She was trying to go straight. The last thing she needs right now is any more trouble of any sort. If we tell Social Services, the whole thing becomes official. And once that happens it can never be kept quiet again. They might even take the baby off her.'

'I don't think— Liam, we must tell them!'

'No. It would complicate things so much. If we can just keep quiet about this for a couple of days—a week at most. Just until I can find Lucy, get her sorted out.'

Turning in his seat, he reached for Peta's hands, held them in both of his, gripping her fingers tightly as he looked deep into her face.

'Peta—please! Please help me with this!'

It shocked her rigid. And it shocked her into silence. 'Please,' he had said. *'Please.'* And not just once, but twice in quick succession.

And this husband of hers never, ever said please.

He hadn't even said please on the day that he had asked her to marry him.

Oh, he used the word in an everyday sort of way—the thoughtless, almost meaningless 'pleases' and 'thank-yous' that peppered everyone's speech in the shops, in a restaurant or on the phone. But a real, true *please*, the sort that meant, *I need this thing so much, and you are the only person who can provide it for me,* that was one word that never passed his lips.

'It means that much to you?'

He didn't have to answer. That 'please' had told her all she needed to know. But still he nodded his dark head.

'Just give me a few days to make some enquiries. Will you stay that long?'

'Stay?'

For a moment her thoughts went blank. She had completely forgotten her pretend threat to leave—to divorce him. But Liam, it seemed, remembered everything.

'You want me to stay for the baby?'

The thought that that was all had the force of a brutal kick from a horse's hoof, bruising her soul in an instant.

'For that if nothing else.'

'And what do you want?'

'You know what I want. What I've always wanted. The marriage that we agreed to at the beginning. Marriage on the terms we arranged a year ago.'

'Marriage and a child.' It was just a husky-voiced whisper, her voice unravelling round the edges.

'A legitimate child.'

The hard, unyielding tone was back, and she knew that there was no way she could reach behind that expression of total imperviousness to anything softer, more approachable underneath.

'"No child, no marriage",' she quoted bitterly.

Liam made no response but simply regarded her unblinkingly, no flicker of emotion in the green depths of his eyes.

'So what is this, Liam? Are you keeping Alice here in an attempt to make me feel clucky and maternal—to get my biological clock ticking away?'

A look of scorching contempt seared over her from her head to her feet, making her toes curl in painful response to the blaze of its cynical derision.

'Clucky?' he echoed savagely. 'You?'

It stung like the flick of a whip, pushing her into an unthinking response.

'I could be! I would be—with the right person.'

She recognised her mistake as soon as she had spoken. The words fell into a terrible, stark silence. A silence so saturated with tension that the air seemed to be thick with it, making it impossible to breathe.

'The right person,' Liam echoed dangerously. 'And the "right person", of course, would not be me.'

Peta closed her eyes in an agony of regret at what she had said. 'With the right person' had meant with someone who loved her, with someone who could offer her a lifetime's commitment. But it had come out all wrong, and she knew that Liam was thinking of her furious declaration that no money he offered he would be enough to persuade her to have his child and combining it dangerously with what she had just said. And the explosive potential of those two declarations made her blood turn to ice just to think of it.

'I…' she began, not knowing what to say, only knowing she had to try and defuse the ticking time bomb she had inadvertently set off. 'I didn't…'

But when she opened her eyes again she found that she was talking to thin air. In the moment that she had been sightless Liam had got to his feet, stalking from the room without a single word to her.

For the second time in less than twelve hours Liam found that walking from the room was a far wiser bet than staying in it.

He didn't trust himself to face Peta any longer until he had got himself back under control, rein in the anger that was threatening to break free of the restraints he had imposed on it and do more damage than he could possibly imagine. If he so much as opened his mouth, then he knew he would not be able to stop, and he already had more

than enough problems to deal with, without adding more
as a result of his own foolishness.

A shower might do the trick. A very hot shower—followed by a punishing cold one.

It didn't work. By the time he was back in the bedroom,
towelling himself dry again, his teeth were chattering, his
skin tingling so hard that it almost burned, but in his mind
there was still just the icy flame of dark, savage anger that
it seemed nothing could suppress.

It was as he tossed the jeans that he had worn that day
into the wash basket that an unexpected rustling sound
caught his attention, making him snatch them back up
again in curiosity. A check through the pockets revealed
the small slip of tablets that he had taken from Peta, here,
in their bathroom this morning.

'I couldn't bring a baby into this world—your world…
I could never have a child in a loveless marriage.'

The words she had flung at him now echoed round in
his head, replacing the purely physical cold with the freez-
ing burn of pure anger.

'I could be! I would be—with the right person.'

Hellfire!

His hand clenched on the strip of tablets, crushing them
ferociously. He had given the woman everything he had
promised—everything she had wanted!—and in return she
had thrown it all right back in his face.

Well, he would show her. If she wanted to fight fire
with fire, then so would he. But the fire he had in mind
was of a very different, very much more pleasurable sort.

For a long, silent moment he contemplated the package
of tablets in his hand. Only two had been taken. But there
would be more somewhere.

A careful hunt through the drawers in Peta's dressing
table revealed what he was looking for, bringing a grim

smile of satisfaction to his face. There was just one more thing…

A couple of minutes later he was heading back down the stairs, more than ready for a fight.

Peta was still sitting exactly where he had left her, her hands clasped in her lap as she stared into the fire which had now burned down to just brightly glowing embers. Even the bowl of soup and the plate of sandwiches, already beginning to look dried up and unappetising, still stood on the table just as he had left them some time before.

She glanced up swiftly as soon as he walked into the room, then immediately dropped her eyes again and fixed them on a point on the rug at her feet.

'Your soup's gone cold.'

It was all Peta could manage. The long minutes she had spent just sitting, waiting for Liam's return, had been the worst sort of endurance test. One that had stretched her nerves to breaking point.

From the moment that he had stalked out of the room she had been struggling against a craven response to run. The weaker part of her nature desperately wanted to go—grab her coat and get out of there, never have to face Liam again. But as soon as she considered the idea the stronger side of her had rejected it out of hand. For one thing there was Alice to consider; she couldn't just abandon the little girl when Alice's mother had already done that. And, besides, she had never been a quitter. No matter what the problem, she stayed and fought. Though this time she didn't see any possibility of either of them winning.

'I'm not hungry,' Liam responded brusquely. 'At least, not for food.'

She didn't need to ask what his hunger was for. It was there in the burn of his eyes, the slight sensual droop to the corners of his heavy eyelids that gave him a sultry, sexual appeal that went straight to her heart.

At any other time she would have responded instantly to that appeal. And even now her body ached with the longing to go into his arms, to drown in his kisses, to abandon herself to the need that simply being with him always created in her. But if she did that then she would be right back at square one, having lost all the ground that she had gained over the past day.

Or was the fact that she had lost ground today rather than gaining it?

If the truth was told, she no longer even knew just what was winning and what was losing. Was staying with Liam while knowing that he didn't love her the worst thing that could happen? Or was the most terrible prospect ahead of her the thought of ending their pretence of a marriage and then living alone, never seeing the man she loved again?

'There's nothing else on offer.'

'No?' he questioned silkily. 'I wonder how long you can keep that up? Doesn't the phrase cutting off your nose to spite your face seem to apply here?'

Not even troubling to reply, Peta simply flashed him a look of pure scorn, praying that it hid the suspicion and doubt that was troubling her. Just what was going through Liam's scheming, manipulative mind now?

She soon found out.

Prowling across the room with an easy, loping stride, he came to stand at the side of her chair.

'Here…'

He held out his left hand, palm uppermost and flat. In the middle of it gleamed the brilliance of a bright solitaire diamond, the mellow beauty of gold.

Her wedding and engagement rings.

She swallowed hard, forced out a response.

'And what am I supposed to do with those?' The fight

she was having to ensure that her voice didn't quaver made it sound brittle and cold instead.

'You could try wearing them. I bought them for you.'

It sounded so simple, so totally reasonable, and yet she knew that, this being Liam, it couldn't ever be like that. There was so much else behind it.

'And *I* gave them back to you. I don't want them.'

The lie caught in her throat. She wanted those rings with all her heart. It had meant so much to her to be able to wear them. To know that she was Liam's wife. But that had been before she had realised that she needed so much more than he could give. That she could never continue with the sort of marriage that was all he had to offer. That being with him and knowing that he didn't love her was more than she could bear.

She had prayed that he might love her. And then, when it had become obvious that that particular request was never going to be answered, she had prayed instead that she could *stop* loving him. Only to find that that had proved equally impossible.

'I don't want them, Liam!'

'Well, neither do I.'

With a quick movement of his hand, he tipped the rings out of his palm and onto the coffee-table, where they bounced once, rolled an inch or two and then lay still, two beautiful but meaningless symbols of a love that had never existed.

'And we can do without these...'

Peta couldn't see the first thing he tossed onto the fire, only the sudden flare of exotically coloured flame as the heat took hold and incinerated whatever it was. But the next item was in a cardboard package; a box that smouldered for a vital couple of seconds before the singed ends split apart and it too burst into flames. And in those seconds she could read what was printed on the packaging.

'That's my Pill!'

Pushing herself out of her chair, she tried to reach him before he tossed the other two packages after the first. But she was just seconds too late, and even as she stooped, attempting to snatch them back before the flames engulfed them, Liam caught hold of her hands, strong fingers closing tightly around her wrists, and pulled her back out of harm's way.

'Don't be bloody stupid!' he snarled. 'You could have burned yourself!'

'I don't care!' she flung back. 'I need those pills—I—'

'No you don't,' Liam put in with deadly calm, stopping her dead and driving all the fight from her in a rush. 'You won't be needing any contraceptive pills,' he repeated, driving the point home.

'I—I won't?'

The shake of his head was as harshly adamant as his expression, no hint of any chink in his armour of obdurate rejection of her hesitant question.

'There'll be no point to taking anything like that from now on. Either you stay in this marriage, in which case you sleep with me when I want, every time I want—or you leave, in which case you won't be needing the pills either, because I'll be suing you for divorce. And I swear to God that if you so much as *look* at another man I'll make sure that you never get a single bloody penny from me or from my grandfather's estate if I have to hand it over to the retired racehorses myself.'

Still holding her by the wrists, he swung her round so that she was forced to face him, forced to look into the stony face that no longer bore any resemblance to the man she had loved so desperately.

'So how about it, sweetheart? It's decision time. What do you say? Which way is it going to be?'

# CHAPTER TEN

FOR the space of perhaps a couple of erratic, shaken heartbeats, Peta couldn't believe that she had actually heard what Liam had said correctly. But then, as reality sank in, with reflex action she automatically rejected his outrageous proposal totally out of hand.

'Don't be ridiculous, Liam!' she flung at him. 'Haven't you been listening to a word I said? I don't want this marriage to continue...'

At least not the way it was now.

'I said I wanted...'

'Ah, but that was before you found out just what was in my grandfather's will. I thought that knowing the truth might have helped you see things a little more clearly.'

'Well, you thought wrong. Nothing I've heard or learned has made me change my mind about anything. But it certainly has helped me see one thing a *little more clearly*—and that's you! I've learned that you're a bullying, manipulating, conniving bastard. Someone who thinks only of what he wants and doesn't give a damn about trampling over other people in his way if it means that he can get it.'

'Pots and kettles,' Liam murmured sardonically, the cynical gleam in his eye, the faintly mocking curve to his mouth incensing her further. 'So you don't think that making the decision to go on the Pill and not tell me was a little—*manipulating*. Maybe even conniving?'

Peta opened her mouth to refute the accusation, but an uncomfortably sharp stab from her conscience forced her to rethink immediately. A strong sense of shame, the ad-

135

mission that she was guilty as charged, stopped her from going any further.

'I would have told you eventually,' was all she managed to mutter.

'Oh, would you?' he returned sceptically. 'And precisely when was that going to be? When you tired of what our marriage brought you—or when my grandfather died and you realised that there wasn't as much for you in this as you first thought?'

'It wasn't like that!'

'No? So are you going to tell me just what it was like, or do you plan on leaving me to guess?'

Which of course was guaranteed to paralyse her tongue with fear and render her totally speechless, unable to manage a single word.

'Of course not,' Liam drawled cynically. 'Which leaves us right back where we started—your move, darling.'

Her move! She couldn't even think coherently, let alone form a reasonable response.

Liam made a show of consulting his watch and noting the time.

'I'll give you five minutes to decide. Either you stay or you go. You just have to decide what you want from this marriage and our future.'

'Do we have one?'

She had to struggle to raise her voice above a whisper, and the effort made it crack embarrassingly in the middle.

'Do we have a future?'

Liam made a pretence of actually considering her question, then he lifted his shoulders in another of those carelessly dismissive shrugs that expressed his total indifference to anything she might say or feel.

'That really rather depends on you. I've told you where I stand—I want a child. And I don't have time to waste on this. Because my grandfather isn't exactly a patient man. Unless he has some news of a baby on the way pretty soon, I reckon he'll go ahead and cut me out of his will anyway. And then we'll both be dropped right in it. And right now the only candidate I have for the mother of that child is you.'

'Well, you certainly can't imagine that I'd want to sleep with you now, after what you've done.'

Her wild gesture indicated the fire, where the last remains of the tablet box was now crinkling into thin black ash and then totally disintegrating once and for all.

'It'd be like playing Russian roulette with my future.'

'So now you know how it feels. You had a metaphorical gun pointed at my head when you decided to start taking the Pill and lying to me about it.'

'I never lied!' Peta said miserably.

'Oh, no, of course not,' Liam snarled. 'I'm sorry—you didn't actually *lie* about it—you just neglected to tell me the truth. Same difference. Either way, you took my future out of my hands for your own ends. But now I'm taking it right back. So it's up to you. Either you stay or you go—but believe me, sweetheart, you walk out that door and you're gone for good. You never, ever walk back in.'

'I can't stay!'

'Then go.'

Liam swung away, marched to the door, wrenched it open, then stood there, waiting.

'Come on, Peta—there's nothing in your way. I certainly won't stop you.'

Was he mad? he asked himself. Was he totally out of what little was left of his mind? He'd decided that he wanted her to stay. That he wanted her here, with him, no matter what. And now he was offering her the chance to leave. Was he really going to stand there and just watch as she walked past him, out of the door and out of his life?

She wouldn't go. That was the truth of it.

She wouldn't go because she would lose so much if she did. If she had married him only for his money—the money she thought his grandfather was going to leave to him—then she had no option but to stay. She thought she'd get nothing any other way.

But if she walked it meant the money wasn't her only motivation. If she stayed then he knew exactly where he stood—which was precisely nowhere. Nowhere except as an income provider. A way of keeping his greedy, grasping wife in the manner to which she had happily become accustomed.

Oh, hell, he could live with that. He'd have to. It would be all that was on offer. Face facts, he *had* lived with it this past year, and he'd been quite content with it. But that had been before he'd begun to allow himself the prospect of even considering the possibility that there could be more. Before he'd started to consider the reality of sharing a life with Peta—a future—a child.

Before he had started to worry that if he couldn't give her the child that she wanted then their marriage was doomed before it had even started.

'Well? You said you wanted to leave. Are you going?'

Perhaps, deep down, he really wanted her to call his bluff. He wanted her to defy him, march right past him and out into the night. Because that would mean there was more to her than the simple greed he suspected drove all her actions.

Okay, so if she left now, then he would have a fight on his hands. He would have to let her go, let her hate him for a while, at least until he got a few other things sorted out. Until he found Lucy, for one, and got her and her baby back together. By then maybe Peta would have calmed down and she would listen. They could start talking—really talking.

He could tell her how it had made him feel to think of their child—more, of the prospect of the two of them raising it. Of working together to care for it, providing a future for their baby and in the process creating a future for themselves. How he had never before ever thought in terms of words like a lifetime or for ever, but had come to realise that he could actually want them after all. How he could have had a child with any woman at any stage of his life, but he had come to realise that the only woman he wanted as the mother of his child was her.

And he would have told her that if only his fear of being sterile hadn't got in the way.

So now he could only be thankful that he hadn't spoken. Because only now would he know by the way she chose, exactly what she really felt about him.

'Your time's almost up, darling. You have fifty seconds left.'

Peta almost made it.

She was on her way to the door, had actually nerved herself to go. In spite of the tears that burned at her eyes, blurring her vision so that she almost blundered into a chair on her way across the room, she knew that she couldn't bear to stay. She couldn't take any more. She had to go—to get away—to snatch a little time to be by herself, to draw breath, lick her wounds in peace, hide…

But then a small murmuring sigh from the makeshift cot caught her attention and held her back.

And in the space of a single, shuddering heartbeat she knew she was lost.

She could walk out for her own sake. In fact, she knew she would do so much better to turn on her heel and go without even a backward glance. All the rules of self-preservation demanded it, and her own common sense urged her on to take the one positive action she could. She could even walk away from Liam, though it tore at her heart to do so. She couldn't give him what he wanted, couldn't be the undemanding, uncommitted wife he was looking for. She couldn't make him happy, and so she would do better not even to try and stay where she didn't belong.

But Alice was quite a different matter.

Could she really walk out and leave the little baby girl all alone? All right, so she wouldn't be totally alone. She would have Liam with her. But while she was sure that Liam would do his best, that he would care for the baby as well as he possibly could, that still didn't ease Peta's conscience enough to leave her free to go.

Even in the few short hours she had spent with the little girl, feeding her and changing her and cuddling her through the long lonely hours of the afternoon, she had developed a bond with the infant that she couldn't even think of trying to break. Not until she could put Alice back in her mother's arms again. The baby needed a female presence in her life. Tiny as she was, she must be missing the warmth and security of her mother's arms, and Peta had vowed that until her mother was found she would provide the love and security the little girl needed.

Besides, if she didn't stay then who would look after Alice in order to give Liam the freedom to go out hunting for her missing mother as he had said that he would as soon as daylight dawned?

'Come on, darling.' Liam's taunting voice reached her through the veil of misery that filled her head. 'What are you waiting for?'

'I—I'm not going.'

It was low, despondent, barely a whisper, and he must have had to strain to hear it. But she still wasn't sure whether he hadn't in fact caught the words or whether he was just rubbing in his victory and her sense of defeat when he asked, 'What was that, sweetheart? What did you say?'

'I said I'm not going!'

This time it was high and tight, shrill with the fight she was having with herself not to break down and admit that he had her trapped.

'I'm not going! I can't—I won't! I have to stay.'

'I thought you'd see sense—realise what side your bread was buttered...'

'No! It isn't like that. It *isn't!*' she repeated emphatically when she saw the disbelieving sidelong glance he turned on her. 'I'm not staying for me or for you, but for—for Alice's sake.'

'Of course,' Liam murmured, every syllable implying disbelief, totally refuting her reasons for staying.

'Of course!'

Peta actually stamped her foot hard on the thick carpet to make her point.

'I'm not staying because I want to be here with you, or because of the prospect of your inheritance, or any such thing. I'm staying because Alice needs me and that's the only reason. So if you're harbouring any thoughts of getting me back into your bed because of this then I suggest you clear them out of your nasty, sordid little mind—and fast! Our marriage is over—done with—particularly that side of it! I wouldn't sleep with you again if you offered me your grandfather's fortune on a plate!'

'No?'

'No!'

'Well, we'll just have to see.'

Liam stretched lazily, flexing tight shoulder muscles, and raked a hand through his hair.

'You see, I'm afraid I can't promise to keep to your terms. You may think that our marriage is over, but I don't agree.'

Reaching out, he pushed the door to again. The slam of wood against wood as it closed firmly sounded ominous and portentous in Peta's sensitised ears. It was a sound of decision, a full stop, marking the ending of one phase and the beginning of another—one from which there was no possible chance of turning back, no matter how much she might want to.

'I married you because I wanted you more than any other woman I'd ever met in my whole life, and nothing has changed. In spite of everything that's happened, I still want you—more than ever, if that were possible. I ache just to look at you...'

'Well, then, you'll just have to ache...'

Peta tried for defiance but it faded into obvious bluster as he strolled towards her, silent and intent and as arrogant as a hunting cat. And she was his prey. Just the thought of it made her heart clench, drying her throat on a shiver of fearful apprehension.

He smiled, and she hated that smile on sight. There was no warmth in it, no gentleness, no softening of his expression at all. The cold, cruel light in his eyes had strengthened, holding her transfixed, like a small, terrified rabbit caught in the headlights of an oncoming car.

'Oh, no, sweetheart—there's no "have to" about this. You've laid down terms—but I choose to ignore them. In spite of all your protestations, I will have you again.'

'You won't! I...'

She looked deep into his polished jade eyes, saw the coldly unwavering intent that burned there and a spasm of fear clenched her stomach.

'You're not thinking... You can't...!'

'No, I can't,' he agreed, the malevolent widening of that smile telling that he understood only too well the fear that lay behind her instinctive protest. 'But I won't have to. Believe me, darling, I won't even need to think of taking you by force. It won't be necessary.'

'Ne—' Peta couldn't believe what she was hearing, and she could hardly choke out her stunned echoing of his words. 'Necessary?'

'We are man and wife,' Liam murmured with deadly softness, and to Peta's shock he reached out a long, powerful finger and touched it to her mouth, making her realise how her lips had fallen open, parting in an expression of total shock.

'Man and wife,' he repeated, watching every tiny response, every fleeting flicker of emotion that played across her face as he traced the soft outline of her mouth with infinite gentleness, stroking the smooth skin with a tenderness that wrenched at her heart with its cruel deceit.

'We—we may be man and—and wife…' she managed. 'But that doesn't mean you can demand your—your…'

'My conjugal rights?' he enquired silkily, when words failed her and she stumbled to a clumsy halt. 'Oh, Peta, can't you see that's not what I mean at all?'

'It's not?'

A tiny flare of hope leapt in her heart as he shook his burnished head, only to be totally extinguished in the moment that he answered her question.

'I won't need to *demand* anything. There'll be no reason to. What I want you'll give me willingly—all that I want and more. You'll come to me of your own choice.'

'Never!'

'Oh, yes you will, sweetheart.'

Never before had she hated that 'sweetheart' quite as much as now, when it was spoken with such a warmth, with such a loving emphasis, when she knew without hope that he was lying through his teeth.

'You'll come to me because you can't help yourself.

Because we were made to be together. Because I am the man for you just as you are the woman for me.'

'No.'

Desperately she shook her head, sending her dark hair flying out in a perfumed cloud around her pale face.

*'No!'*

The man for you! If only he knew! If only he realised just how much she felt for him. That he was her soul mate, her one and only, the love of her lifetime. But if he recognised that then he would have a hold over her that he would use quite mercilessly. He would turn it against her, use it for his own ends—and when he was done...

When he was done would he discard her without a second thought, casting her aside like a broken toy that a spoiled child had tired of, wanting something new? She didn't know. She only knew that if he took her love and used it to get what he desired then he might just as well throw her away when he'd had what he wanted. There wouldn't be anything left of her anyway, just a ruined, empty husk that had been sucked dry of all that was good in it.

'Yes,' Liam insisted, and to her horror there was laughter in his voice.

It was laughter that, like his smile earlier, held no warmth, no genuine amusement. He was laughing at her not with her, and as she stared at him in confusion he smiled again, with malign gentleness.

'You will come to me, darling, I know you will. And how do I know this? Because we are man and wife and we have been so for the past twelve months. And believe me, I've put that year together to good use. If I've made love to you once in that time, I must have done it a thousand times. I know you, my sweet wife. I know everything about you when you're in bed with me. I know how you close your eyes when I kiss you...'

Bending his dark head, he took her lips in a long, slow, sultry kiss. And, knowing that his eyes were on her all the time, glittering green burning into vulnerable blue, Peta struggled to defy him. She tried desperately to keep her eyes open, to meet him stare for stare, but even as she thought she had succeeded he adjusted his mouth a little, let the tip of his tongue run along the faint opening of her lips, and with a groan of defeat she let her eyelids flutter closed.

'I know how your body responds to mine,' he whispered against her mouth, running his hands down her back and drawing her closer.

So close that he had to be aware of the shudder of response that ran through her, the immediate quickening race of her pulse, the pounding of her heart. A pounding that lurched unevenly as that wickedly knowing hand slid up again to cup and hold one of her breasts under the soft lavender sweater.

'I know what turns you on, darling. And I shall use it. We're lovers, Peta…'

'We *were* lovers,' she croaked, knowing she didn't sound in the least bit convincing. 'It's in the past, Liam.'

'In the past?' he echoed incredulously. 'Sweetheart, you know you don't really mean that. How can you mean it when your kiss tells me the opposite, when your heart is racing here, against mine, when your breast fits into my hand as if it was made for it—when it swells to greet my touch…?'

'No!'

With a violence that wrenched at her soul as much as her body, she pulled herself away from the enticing temptation of his embrace, the force of her movement flinging her halfway across the room.

'No! I won't let you—this isn't going to happen! It can't happen.'

The ultimate horror was Liam's lack of reaction, his relaxed, impassive calm. His eyes told her that he was unconcerned by her reaction, that it didn't worry him at all. That he knew she was running scared and he didn't have to do anything more to prove it. She had done that all for herself.

'It will happen, darling. There's no doubt about that. The only question is when. But I'm in no hurry. After the banquet I enjoyed last night, I'm not exactly hungry yet.'

The fiendishly gleaming green-eyed gaze dropped to the rug before the fire, and when he glanced up again she knew without a word being spoken that he was thinking of their wildly passionate lovemaking right there, before the fire, on their return from the party.

'I can take my time. I can wait for you to come to me, to ask for me. I reckon it'll be worth the wait.'

'Then you'll wait till the end of the world.'

She was still speaking when he shook his head again, outrageously looking almost sorrowful at the thought of how little, in his opinion, she knew herself.

'I think not, sweetheart. If you like, I'll have a little wager with you. It's Christmas Eve the day after tomorrow. I'll bet that before midnight strikes to turn the Eve into Christmas Day itself you'll come to me and beg me to take you. And I'll be only too happy to do exactly as you want.'

His beautiful mouth curved into a wide, devilish grin that froze the blood in her veins.

'We'll call it my Christmas present, shall we?'

# CHAPTER ELEVEN

'I'M GOING to bed.'

Peta had held out as long as she possibly could, but she couldn't stay up for ever. It was getting late, her eyes were beginning to close and she could feel herself drifting off as she sat in her chair by the fire. She knew she had no alternative but to make a move, and so she stood up and turned to Liam, her blue eyes wary.

In the beginning it had all seemed so easy. All she had to do was to keep well away from Liam, never let him touch her. Certainly never let him kiss her, and she would be safe. And for a time that had seemed perfectly easy to do.

The practical matters involved in looking after Alice and making sure she was warm, fed, and comfortable offered plenty of opportunities to keep busy, concentrating her attention on the little girl. So she had been able to get through what was left of the rest of the day without ever having too much time alone in the same room with Liam. But all the same she had felt as if she were walking on eggshells, never quite sure which way he was going to jump—and when.

'I think that's a good idea,' was his even-toned response. 'You look worn out.'

He didn't make any sort of a move, didn't even put aside the book he had been reading. Could it really be that simple?

'Shall I carry Alice up for you?'

They had agreed during the evening that Alice would be best left in her drawer 'cot' and that they would bring it up to the bedroom for the night. Tomorrow, if nothing happened to reunite the little girl with her birth mother, they would see about getting something more suitable for her to sleep in.

'I'd appreciate that. Thanks.'

She had never hurried up the wide, curving staircase so fast. It seemed that with every step she took she was reminded of times, too many to count, during the past year, when she had led him, or he had led her, up these stairs and into the bedroom where...

Her mind hazed over, refusing to remember the heated, erotic exchanges, the lingering kisses, the sighs, the wonderful violence of the orgasms that had seemed to make her mind explode in delight.

Those times were past, she told herself, refusing to listen to the protests of a heart that couldn't bear to consider the prospect of 'never again', the thought of the emptiness of the life that lay ahead.

And what would be so wrong about giving in? A wanton little voice insinuated into her thoughts. What have you to lose?

Everything! She told her tormentor sharply. My self-esteem, for one, my pride. I've lived for months now with the knowledge that this man—my husband—doesn't love me. That was bad enough. But now I find that he doesn't trust me either. That he truly believes that all I want him for is his money—and that he despises and hates me for that. The lack of love I might have learned to accept. But how can I live with—how can I give myself to a man whose only feelings for me are contempt and abhorrence—and lust for my body?

She might just as well be that brood mare she had described herself as to Liam only that morning.

'If you put Alice there, by the bed,' she said, marvelling at the way her voice sounded almost normal, even as her mind and heart were being torn so agonisingly in two, 'I'll be sure to hear her if she cries.'

She fled into the bathroom as he was settling the little girl, waiting what she thought was a safe enough time before she emerged, fully expecting that Liam would by now be back downstairs.

He wasn't.

Instead he was still in the room, on the far side of the bed—his side. He had already stripped off his shirt and sweater, kicked away his shoes, and as Peta watched in disbelief and horror he sat on the edge of the bed in order to take off his socks.

'What do you think you're doing?'

Dark amusement gleamed in the eyes he turned in her direction.

'I would have thought that was obvious. I'm getting ready for bed.'

'Not here…'

Instinctively she wrapped the ice-blue robe even more closely round her, yanking the belt tight at her waist. The matching nightdress she wore underneath was far too revealing for comfort.

'And where else would I sleep? This is my bedroom.'

'Yes, but…'

'Peta, I'm tired; we both are. It's been a long day.'

That careful, resigned patience could grate very quickly, Peta decided, particularly when it was so obviously an act.

'I'm ready to sleep.'

'But not here!'

She didn't trust him if he got into bed—their marriage bed—with her. She didn't trust herself, come to that!

'I'm sleeping here!'

'And so am I.'

Standing up again, he dropped his hands to the leather

belt around his narrow waist, began to unfasten the buckle.

'Liam!'

The gleam in the moss-green eyes grew brighter, his smile taunting her.

'Peta!' he mimicked her tone mercilessly. 'Why are you behaving like an outraged virgin who has never had a man in her bedroom when we both know that that is so very far from the truth?'

The crazy thing was that she *felt* like an outraged virgin. She hadn't even felt this nervous on their wedding night, and on that first night they had slept together she had been so totally lost in her hunger for him that she hadn't even noticed—or cared—which room they were in.

'I thought I'd made my feelings plain.'

Was that cold, stiff, stilted little voice really hers? She winced inside, hearing the way she sounded.

'I don't intend to sleep with you. I consider that our marriage is over, for good.'

'And I thought I'd made *my* feelings plain. Our marriage is over when I say so and not before. And I will sleep wherever I want.'

'Not with me, you won't. If you're going to sleep here then I'll find somewhere else.'

Snatching up the sleeping baby, drawer and all, she made her way out of the room and down the landing. She didn't know if she could escape, but maybe if she could just get into another room...

She never made it. She was still fumbling awkwardly with the door one-handed, as she tried to balance her burden and avoid disturbing Alice, when a pair of warm, muscular arms snaked round her waist and closed tight.

'We are still husband and wife,' Liam murmured against her ear, his breath warm on her cheek. 'And husbands and wives sleep together.'

'No…'

'Yes. Don't fight it, sweetheart. You know you can't win. And besides, you don't want to waken Alice.'

That last comment gave her the excuse she desperately needed. She didn't want to admit, even to herself, the way that her body had responded instantly and fiercely to just the touch of his. She wanted to ignore the tiny explosions of need that had been set off along every nerve path as she felt the heat of his flesh surround her, the strength of his chest against her back. The clean, faintly musky scent of his skin tantalised her nostrils, and low-down in her body she could feel the burn of primitive need uncoiling like a hungry snake, stretching, demanding.

'No,' she managed unsteadily. 'I don't want to wake the baby.'

Releasing his tight hold around her waist, Liam slowly turned her in the circle of his arms. As she came face to face with him he took the cumbersome drawer in which Alice still slept peacefully from her and held it securely under one arm before he turned his attention to his wife.

And what he saw shocked him badly.

At the sight of the pallor of Peta's cheeks, the deep, dark shadowed pools that were her eyes, Liam felt his conscience reproach him. She looked done in, half-dead on her feet. And perhaps it was no wonder. Alice had not given them an easy afternoon. She had fussed and fretted, probably missing her mother. The bottle that Peta had prepared had been rejected at first, and only finally accepted with a lot of gentle coaxing and encouragement. But even when fed the little girl had refused to settle. It had taken a lot of nursing, cuddling, rocking in Peta's arms, before she had finally stopped crying and succumbed to the tiredness that had overwhelmed her.

And now Peta looked as if she was ready to do the same. As if she was about to keel over where she stood.

'You look worn out.'

Her only response was a small, silent nod. The movement made her hair fall forward over her face, and as she lifted a hand to push it back she suddenly seemed very young, very innocent, very, very feminine. Everything that was masculine in him responded at once, wanting to hold and protect her, to care for her to the limits of his strength.

It was the return of a feeling that had plagued him all day. It had started in the moment that he had first come back to the house and seen her feeding the baby. It had brought home to him how much he had always wanted a family of his own, the dream he had thought he had fulfilled when he had married Peta.

And that feeling wouldn't go away. Foolishly, weakly, he had let it linger, allowing himself the comfort of this brief interlude if he couldn't have the real thing. It was Christmas and he still had his wife and a baby in the house, even if, with a terribly black irony, the baby wasn't his and his wife planned to leave him just as soon as she could.

'You did well today,' he said quietly. 'You're a natural.'

The words seemed to hang before their eyes, suspended in the air between them, and Peta suddenly found that her gaze was swimming with tears. The new gentleness in Liam's tone was almost her undoing. Biting her lip, she blinked hard to force the stinging moisture back.

'Now come to bed. It's late. We both need sleep.'

'Sleep!'

She couldn't help it. Shock and mystified disbelief drove the exclamation from her in an undignified squawk of surprise.

'*Sleep?*'

'Of course.'

His look of wide-eyed innocence was almost perfect, only spoiled by the wickedly dancing gleam he couldn't totally suppress.

'What else did you think I had in mind?'

She didn't need to answer that, so instead she contented herself with turning on him the most fulminating glare she could conjure up, praying that it hid both the astonishment and the yearning that she knew must be just under the surface.

And then Liam pulled the rug right out from under her, devastating her, making her feel as if the world had suddenly shifted and her feet were no longer secure on the ground as she had believed.

'Come with me, wife,' he said softly. 'Come to bed and sleep with me. Nothing more, I promise you. Not tonight. We've both had enough of today. Tomorrow may be different—but let's wait and see. We'll let tomorrow bring what it will. Tonight we'll just sleep together. Truly sleep.'

He held out his hand to her, and when she put hers into it he led her back to their bedroom. Setting down Alice's makeshift cot, he pulled back the covers from the bed and smoothed down the sheet. With hands that were supremely gentle, and strangely non-sexual, he eased the silk robe from her and tossed it aside.

'Now, get into bed.'

A light but firm pressure on her shoulders pushed her down onto the mattress and Liam watched as she curled her legs up, let her head drop on the pillows. Just for a moment he stood looking down at her, then one strong hand smoothed the dark hair away from her brow.

'Sleep well.'

To her astonishment she felt a single soft kiss on her brow, then he moved away. As she lay there, her eyes growing heavy, she heard the sounds of him moving about in the bathroom, the running of water. She was already drifting away on a heavy tide of sleep when he came back and slid in beside her, but she struggled to wake just a little to…

'Goodnight, sweetheart,' Liam said gently, and maybe it was the fact that her brain wasn't quite focused, or the softness of his voice deceiving her, but this time she could catch nothing of the darkly satirical emphasis with which he usually coloured the affectionate word. Instead it seemed open, straightforward—even honest.

And it was with that word in her head, and the feel of Liam's arms coming round her, warm and strong and protective, drawing her into the heat of his body, that she drifted asleep and knew nothing until deep into the night.

When Alice's hungry cries broke the stillness of the dark, she surfaced from a long way down, struggling awake with an effort. Rubbing her eyes with the back of her hand, she pushed herself upright, reaching automatically for her robe.

'It's all right, little one, I'm here.'

She had the baby in her arms when she realised that the space in the bed beside her was empty. And even as she pushed her thoughts round to the idea of going downstairs, warming a bottle, Liam was coming back into the room, bringing the feed the baby wanted with him.

'I heard her starting to get restless a few minutes ago,' he explained. 'The milk was ready—all I had to do was warm it. It's my turn anyway. Here—give her to me.'

He'd been like this during the day, Peta reflected, watching as he took the baby into his arms and offered the bottle to her. In spite of the tensions between them, he had been scrupulously fair about taking his turn with either feeding or changing the baby. Never once had he held back or hesitated, or made any suggestion that caring for Alice was women's work and not his sort of thing.

She couldn't drag her eyes away from the sight of Liam, propped up against the pillows, his broad, hair-hazed chest bare, the navy pyjama trousers the only covering he wore. His head was bent over the baby in his arms; his attention totally focused on her small, upturned face.

And now, when she wasn't able to cope with it, came the memory of the way, as she drifted asleep, she had curved her back against Liam and felt the hard, potent pressure against her buttocks that told of his hunger for her. And yet he hadn't acted on it, had made no overt moves, hadn't even kissed her, but had simply let her rest.

'So I get the nappy this time—thanks!'

Somehow she managed to inject a thread of humour into a voice that didn't sound like her own, knowing that she was trying to distract herself from the erotic thoughts her memory was throwing up at her. Memories that were even harder to dispel when Liam looked up sharply, green eyes locking with blue over the baby's head, before he flashed her a devastating smile.

'You know what we agreed. Share and share alike. I did the nappy before we put her to bed. You have that pleasure now.'

Was this what he would be like with his own child? Peta couldn't help wondering, wincing inwardly at the bitter stab of distress that idea brought.

What would Liam think, what would he say if he knew that at times during the evening she had allowed herself to drift into a world of the imagination? That she had let the comforting illusion that she and Liam were together, caring for Alice, slip into her mind, where it had taken root in a dangerous way?

Leaning forward, she stroked the baby's hand with one gentle finger, smiling in sudden delight as the chubby fist closed round her.

'We'll need to get some more nappies in tomorrow. And more milk—plus some other bits and pieces in case she has to stay with us for a while. Would it be too extravagant to buy her a proper cot?'

'Not at all. A little lady like Alice can't sleep in a drawer except as a make do for one night. And when we find her mother, then we can give her the cot as a present for the baby.'

That 'we' sounded wonderful. Warm and friendly—and so *together* that it made Peta smile just to hear it.

'A Christmas present?'

'No!' It came surprisingly forcefully, startling her. 'It's too practical for a Christmas present. We'll get her some proper gifts too—toys…'

'Liam!' This time her laughter was genuine, unforced. 'She's only a blob! She won't even know it's Christmas.'

'Maybe not—but Alice is my—right now it seems that she might be my only chance to ever have a child to spoil at Christmas, so I'm going to take full advantage. She won't have to accept jumble-sale clothes and shoes as Christmas presents.'

'Jumble…?' Peta echoed, unable to believe what she was hearing.

There was a new note in Liam's voice, a savage, disturbingly vehement intonation in his words, one that told her he was speaking from experience.

'But I thought your mother married…'

'My mother married after my father walked out, yeah…'

Liam reached for a tissue and gently wiped a dribble of milk from the baby's chin.

'And my stepfather had plenty of money—but only for *his* family, not for his wife's bastard-bred mistake.'

The bitterness was so black now that it was obvious he could only be speaking about himself, and it shocked Peta into silence, capable only of listening, unable to express the way her sympathetic heart was aching for the child he had been.

'I got the clothes I needed—the shoes—the food—and that was it. If I asked for anything more I was told I should be grateful that they'd kept me at all—that I wasn't out on the streets with my father where I belonged.'

'No presents at all?'

Liam shook his head roughly, making Alice's big eyes open wide at the sudden movement.

'Sorry, sweetie,' he said gruffly, smoothing a hand over her downy head to calm her. 'I learned not to ask for anything. I knew I wouldn't get it, so it was easier never even to mention it.'

*It was easier never even to mention it.* Just as now it was easier for him never to say please? Never to show how much he wanted something? Peta's conscience gave a tormenting twist, making her shift uneasily under the warm quilt.

'I—I'd like to explain…' she blurted out, hearing the words before she had even realised in her thoughts that she planned to say them. 'About taking the Pill, I mean.'

Liam had been looking down, watching the steady flow of the milk from the bottle as Alice sucked, but at her words his dark gaze flew up again, to fix on her pale face. He didn't say a word, but his silence and a new tension about his long body told her without words being needed that he was listening intently to every word she said.

'I—I didn't lie to you—not at the beginning,' she began hesitantly, wishing she had never started this but knowing that now she had there was no going back. 'I thought that what we had in our marriage was enough. That's because we both wanted children and because there was no one else in our lives we could make it work—I *meant* to make it work!'

'So what happened?' Liam asked when she fell silent, unable to think how to go on, hunting for the right words to explain. 'What changed?'

'I changed—my feelings changed. I—realised that while it might be enough for us, this arrangement we'd made, it—it wasn't good enough for the most important person in all this—a baby.'

Did he understand? Would he understand? He was listening, but did he see what she was trying to say?

'Go on.'

Peta was still struggling to find the way to express what was in her thoughts when Alice wriggled in Liam's arms, waving her tiny hands in the air. At once both Peta's and Liam's gazes were drawn to the little girl, and, watching her, Peta knew how to go on.

'I mean, look at Alice... She's only tiny but she was so restless tonight, it could only be because she missed her mother. And you said—you said that you would do everything you could—anything—to reunite her with her real family.'

Once again his silence told her that he was listening. She kept her eyes fixed on the baby, not daring to look into Liam's face.

'A child deserves parents who love it—and who love each other.'

'I would love my child...'

Liam's protest almost overlaid her words, but not totally. She knew he had heard what she said, knew he was absorbing the implications of it.

'I know you would.'

Her voice was low, dreary, and deep inside her heart was slowly, agonisingly splitting in two. But it had to be said. She meant it so much.

'I know you'd love your child—and so would I. But *we* wouldn't love it together—as one—not as two separate people. And I know you'll understand what I mean. How could you not—with your own experience to draw on? Wouldn't you have been happier as a child if your parents had loved one another?'

'Yeah.' It was gruff, abrupt, as he took the now finished bottle from Alice and propped the baby up on his shoulder, stroking her back with a gentleness that made Peta's already desolated heart break even more.

'So you see what I mean? I came to realise that we could give our child a lot—but we couldn't give him or her the *best*. We couldn't give it two parents who loved one another. Do you understand?'

'Yeah, I understand. You don't have to say anything more. I understand perfectly what you're getting at. And you're right. If we don't even love each other, how could we ever love a child the way it deserves.'

He was sliding off the bed as he spoke, getting to his feet, still with Alice carefully supported on his shoulder, and now he turned towards the door.

'Where are you going?'

She had to force herself to say it, force herself to sound calm and in control, when calm was the very last thing that she felt. For a short time, at least up to the very last minute, some tiny little ray of hope had still lingered deep inside. The hope that he might tell her she was wrong. That he felt more than she believed for her. Or at least that he felt *something*. But how clear did he have to make it to her before her weak, foolish heart accepted there was no chance?

*We don't even love each other.* It couldn't be any more unambiguous than that.

'I thought I'd change Alice's nappy in another room, then make sure she's settled before I put her down to sleep again.'

'But it was my turn—' Peta broke off sharply as Liam lifted a hand to silence her.

'And I'm so wide awake that I won't be able to sleep for some time, so I'll do it—you get some rest.'

It was an order, a command, in a tone that brooked no argument, though Peta opened her mouth to try. But before she could speak Liam had flicked off the light, plunging the room into darkness and effectively ending the conversation. A couple of seconds later even the light from the landing was blocked out as he shut the door firmly behind him, leaving nothing but the tiniest rim of gold at its edge.

She had played her last card, explaining to Liam why she had been taking the Pill. She didn't have anything else left to offer. And she had tried to hint at her feelings with that 'we couldn't give it *two* parents who loved one another'. She was so low, so desperate, that if he had so much as offered her *anything* then she would have taken it. But he hadn't. Instead he'd made it plain that he didn't love her, never would. And he hadn't been able to wait to get out of the room, get away from her and the feelings he didn't want from her.

She had tried everything she could, risked everything she dared—and failed. There was no future for her and Liam. No matter how much she loved him, she had to face the fact that their marriage was over.

'Do you understand?' Liam replayed Peta's words in his head as he closed the bedroom door and headed down the landing. Oh, yes, he *understood* all right! He understood that being married to this wife of his was like riding a wildly out of control rollercoaster. Sweeping up, up, up to something wonderful and spectacular one moment, only to plunge right down to the lowest depths possible the next.

'We couldn't give him or her the *best*...two parents who loved one another.'

Why had this had to happen *now?* Why had she had to come out with that comment on the night when, with the worst possible timing, he had just come to realise what had happened to him? Or rather, when he had just come round to actually putting it into words?

Because it had been creeping up on him for months now. He just hadn't recognised it for what it was because he had no experience with which to compare it, nothing against which to measure it.

He had never truly known about love before.

But love was what had hit him right between the eyes, and he hadn't even seen it coming. He hadn't really believed in it either, always dismissed it as the product of fantasy, the outpourings of romantic, unrealistically idealistic poets, or the cynical manipulations of advertising executives bent on selling schmaltzy cards or dozens of red roses.

It had only been when he had heard the words on his wife's lips that he had had a flash of enlightenment so brilliant, so fierce, that he was surprised that it hadn't lit up the whole of the room—the whole of the house and gardens—in some mad, unbelievable, spectacular firework display.

'We couldn't give him or her...two parents who loved one another.'

Just a single phrase, simple and straightforward. But in the truth that had blazed in Peta's eyes when she'd spoken it he'd seen the death of his hopes and dreams. He had finally come to realise how much he loved his wife, but too late.

With a bitter irony, that realisation had come on the very night that Peta had made it plain that she did not love him.

# CHAPTER TWELVE

CHRISTMAS EVE seemed to have come in the blink of an eye.

When Liam had made his arrogant declaration, setting out his challenge, midnight on Christmas Eve had seemed like a long, long time away, Peta thought. Two whole days—and more.

But she didn't seem to have registered those two days had existed before they had come and gone, and now it was late on the evening of the night before Christmas and she had no idea what was going on in Liam's mind. She was not at all sure just what stage they had reached in her husband's latest campaign to get his way, and she didn't think she even wanted to test out the ground. .

She didn't want to risk rocking the boat in any way whatsoever. In the past forty-eight hours a sort of peace had descended, the kind of truce that she found she could live with and, if not exactly enjoy, then at least manage without breaking down and revealing the way she was disintegrating inside.

Once again it was having Alice with them that saved her. They had spent the first day in the nearest town, shopping for the little girl. At first Peta had tried to be careful, aware of the fact that they might not have Alice for more than a day or so, but Liam had insisted on being hopelessly extravagant, buying everything they could think of and a lot more besides. Bedding, toiletries, clothes, a mobile, toys—all had been piled into the car and taken home with them.

'You know, the baby won't even be interested in some

of these for six months or more.' Peta had laughed as she'd stared at the huge array of parcels and plastic bags that were piled into the little bedroom they had designated 'Alice's room'.

'But she'll enjoy them then,' Liam had returned carelessly. 'When she is ready for them, then they'll be waiting for her.'

He'd been like a child himself, revelling in the choosing and buying of all the brightly coloured delights, Peta reflected now as she sat before the big log fire late on Christmas Eve. And, recalling what he had told her about his own Christmases as a child, the bleakness and misery of knowing that he wasn't wanted, that he was seen only as a burden, who could blame him? But if he was like this now, with a baby who had come into their lives by accident, then how much more would he love being the father of his own child, one that was with him for life and not just a temporary 'loan'?

She was doing the right thing, she told herself, forcing herself to face once again the resolution she had made two nights before. It might break her heart, destroy her hope of happiness, but she was doing the best thing for Liam. Without her, without a wife he could never care for in his life, he would have a chance of starting again. He could meet someone else…marry someone else…have a child with someone else… With someone else she hoped he could be happy, perhaps even in time to meet his grandfather's unreasonable demands.

With someone he really loved.

It was almost too much to bear. With a soft moan she folded her arms around herself, feeling as if she was falling apart inside. The thought of Liam falling in love with someone else was something she had tried to make herself confront ever since she had come to her decision, but each time her mind and heart had flinched away from the prospect, unable to cope with it.

'What are you doing, sitting in the dark?'

Liam had appeared in the doorway behind her and now his hand was on the switch, preparing to flood the room with light.

'No, don't!' Peta protested hastily, terrified that if he did then he would see the marks of tears on her cheeks, know that she had been crying. 'The firelight's lovely—leave it, please.'

'Okay, if that's what you want.'

Liam came to sit beside her on the big settee, leaning back with a sigh of contentment and stretching out his long legs in front of him.

'Alice is fast asleep. And after the amount of milk she downed in that last bottle I'll be very surprised if she wakes for a long time.'

'That would be a welcome change after last night. I think she had us up every hour on the hour. Perhaps she's settling at last. Any news of her mother?'

'None.' Liam shook his head. 'I've drawn a blank everywhere I look. I'm beginning to think she's vanished off the face of the earth. The real problem is that if she's left the village I have no clues as to where to start to look for her. She could go to London—anywhere—and if she disappears into a big city then it could take months to track her down.'

'We're going to have to tell Social Services.'

'I know—but after Christmas. At least we can keep Alice here for the next couple of days.'

And that would give her the excuse to stay until Alice had gone, Peta thought sadly. When the baby was handed over, either to her mother or to official carers, then her reason for staying would also be gone. She would have to leave if she was to give Liam a chance to start again.

But she couldn't think of that now. If she did, it would destroy her. Fixing her eyes on the leaping flames in the hearth, she tried to concentrate on watching the patterns they created, the red glow of the coals.

At the same time she was intensely aware of Liam's physical presence beside her. Dressed entirely in black— black sweatshirt, black jeans—he was a lean, disturbing presence, the faint tang of his aftershave reaching her sensitised nostrils, the sound of his breathing playing havoc with nerves that were constantly attuned to his presence. Every sense she possessed was alert to everything about him.

Nothing had gone as she had expected over the past two days. The truth was that Liam had done the exact opposite of everything she had anticipated. Where she had thought he would flirt and tease her both verbally and physically, use every skill he had to attempt to seduce her, in fact he had kept his distance and made no such move. He had been quiet, reticent, almost distant, and he had barely touched her, making contact only when he absolutely had to, in order to take Alice from her or hand the baby over. Even in bed he'd kept his distance, keeping strictly to his side of the mattress as if he was deliberately avoiding touching her.

And, perversely, the sort of sensory deprivation that he had put her through had had exactly the desired effect he had declared he was aiming for. She missed his touch so badly, missed the feel of his strength close to her in bed, the warmth of his body, the scent of his skin. Her whole being ached with need for him, and the yearning that kept her awake last night had had her tossing and turning in restless misery. She hadn't known that it was possible to feel this lonely even while the person she was missing so terribly was still in the room.

'What are you thinking?'

Liam's quiet question made her start nervously, turning sharply to find his dark eyes fixed on her face, the flare of the fire mirrored in their smoky depths.

'You've been lost to the world for the last few minutes. It made me wonder just what was going through your mind.'

'Nothing much,' Peta prevaricated.

Desperate to avoid telling him the truth, instead she grasped at the first idea that came into her head, the memory of her thoughts before he had come into the room.

'If you must know, I was thinking about Joshua.'

'About my grandfather? Why was that?'

'I was thinking how mean it was of him to set those conditions on your inheriting Hewland Hall and all the rest of it.'

'He's an old man. Family honour means everything to him. He was never able to forgive my mother for running off and getting pregnant by my father. He desperately wanted a legitimate heir, but I'm the only one he has.'

'But if he hadn't wanted an heir for the estate so much then we might have had a better start. We would have been able to meet and get to know each other without that sense of pressure on us. We could have started completely fresh, without the expectations that he and my parents had.'

Liam's response to her words was total silence. With his face turned towards her, away from the light of the flames, she couldn't read his expression or see what was in his eyes. There was nothing that would give her a clue as to what he was thinking. But then he moved slightly, flexing taut shoulders and running one hand through his hair.

'We still could,' he said quietly.

'Still could?' she echoed, confused. 'Liam…What…?'

But then at last she saw the way his thoughts were

heading, and in the same moment she caught the appeal of the idea, knew a sudden rush of wanting things to be the way he meant. The way she had said would have been better if they had started that way.

Was it possible? Could it really be done? Could they really start afresh, begin as if everything was totally new? Could they act as if they had never met before, as if all the complications and problems that had dogged them had never existed and they were strangers, meeting for the very first time?

'What…?' she began, but Liam forestalled her.

'I'm Liam,' he said, and held out his hand.

For a second she was nonplussed, then she realised and followed his lead.

'Peta—Peta Lassiter.'

Why had she used her maiden name and not her married one? Liam wondered. Perhaps the idea of starting completely afresh, without the mess they had made of their marriage, really appealed to her, as it had appealed to him. But could they do it? How long could they pretend? How long could they keep reality and its disappointments out of this?

For some time, it seemed, as they played the game of being strangers, of finding out about each other as if for the first time. They opened a bottle of wine and sat before the fire and talked.

And talked.

About trivial things at first. About books and films and holidays. About Christmas and celebrations they had known in the past. About presents they had loved, and ones that had been so appalling they just couldn't believe anyone would think they might like them. About how different the festivities had been in America from the ones she had enjoyed at home.

'So left to yourself, then,' Liam said, filling up her glass and then his own before leaning back against the cushions, his long body more relaxed than it had been for days, 'what would you most want for Christmas, if you could have anything you wanted? Anything at all?'

'Anything?' Peta asked, meeting his gaze over the top of her glass.

Something in the way she looked at him made his nerves twist in sudden tension, a tormenting sensation like the prickle of ice-cold pins and needles dancing across his skin. Sitting next to her like this had been a damn stupid mistake. How could he stay so close to her and not touch her, not kiss her?

Each time she moved the gleam of the fire lit up her face, turning the wide, dark eyes to burning flame, glowing on the peachy softness of her skin. The rich cherry velvet dress she had changed into for their meal was long-sleeved, short-skirted, low-necked, supremely feminine. It emphasised the slender length of her legs, the fine bones of her neck and throat. And the warmth of the room released her perfume so that the scent of flowers and the subtle tang of spice assailed his nostrils, tormenting the senses that were already in a state of high alert.

But he had promised himself that he would hold back. That he wouldn't touch her, not unless she gave him some sort of go-ahead. The sex thing was too powerful, too overwhelming between them. They had been caught that way once, and it had got them into this mess. It meant that they had rushed into marriage for all the wrong reasons, and now Peta felt trapped with him, obviously deeply regretting ever having agreed to be his wife when she realised that she could never love him.

'Really anything?'

'Absolutely anything,' Liam confirmed. And, if he could, he would fulfil her dream for her. Even if it was the last thing he could do before she walked out of his life, then he would try.

Did she dare risk it? Peta asked herself. Could she really say what was uppermost in her mind? Could she chance revealing her innermost thoughts and feelings to this man who meant so much to her and yet was still in some ways a mystery?

For several seconds she wavered between yes and no, choosing one and then swinging back to the other. But this was Christmas Eve. A night when magic was supposed to happen. The time when wishes and dreams came true and everyone had a chance at achieving their heart's desire. And as she looked into the deep pools of Liam's eyes she found the phrase 'nothing ventured, nothing gained' repeating over and over inside her head.

'All right...' she said slowly. 'But on one condition.'

'And what's that?'

'You must do the same. If I tell you my dearest wish, then you must tell me yours. No holding back. Do you agree?'

'No holding back,' Liam echoed. 'You have my word on it.'

'All right, then...'

Peta didn't know where to begin. In her mind she tried several different ways of saying it, changing the words around, rephrasing...but still it seemed that there was no way other than just to blurt it right out.

'I wish,' she said, 'that Joshua Hewland wasn't your grandfather! I wish that you weren't the heir to Hewland Hall and the estate and everything! I wish that you were just yourself, with whatever you've earned for yourself, and that nothing came tied up with conditions and promises and the need for legitimate heirs.'

If his silence earlier had shocked her, then this one stretched her nerves to breaking point. It seemed to drag on and on until she was ready to scream—or burst into tears—or both.

'Liam—say something—please.'

At last he stirred, drew in a deep breath.

'Why?' he said, in a voice that didn't seem to belong to him.

'Because I've just—because you…'

'No, I mean why do you wish that? Why is it so important to you?'

Oh, dear Lord! He wanted more from her. And she had used up what little courage she had on her first admission. Did she dare to take it any further?

'Because—because then you might believe that I wanted this marriage for very different reasons than you think. You might understand that the money matters to my parents, but not to me. It was important to them but to me it means nothing. Nothing!'

His stillness and silence seemed almost frightening. He had moved so that his face was in shadow and she couldn't read his expression, couldn't see his eyes. There was no way at all she could know what he was thinking, even begin to interpret just what was going through his mind.

'You want me to believe that?'

All the strength that had given her the power of speech was gone, so all she could do was nod in silent agreement, willing him to trust her as hard as she could.

Another silence, even longer this time. Was he ever going to answer?

At last he sighed.

'You didn't have to tell me.'

'I wanted to…'

'No, I meant you didn't have *tell* me. I worked it out for myself.'

'You did?' Peta couldn't believe what she was hearing.

And now at last Liam turned his face to her and she could see his expression. His smile was crooked, faintly wry—could she dare to think shamefaced?

'Sweetheart, I may be a bit slow on the uptake, but these last couple of days no one could have doubted that when you stayed, you stayed for Alice—to look after her and care for her. And that set me thinking. Looking back at our year together, I realised that although you enjoyed the presents I gave you you never asked for anything, never tried to get more out of me.'

'But you...'

'I know what I said! But I was angry—stupidly out of my head in fury. And so were you. That's why you said you were leaving.'

Peta was grateful for the darkness, the shadows in the room, that hid the way that colour flooded her cheeks. Did he really know her that well?

'Are you telling me you believe me?'

'I'm telling you that you didn't need to explain. That if I'd been anything but a blind, stupid fool, then I would have seen for myself. But I...'

He caught himself up, obviously rethinking what he had been about to say.

'You?'

'Nothing.'

He dismissed her question with a wave of his hand.

'It doesn't matter.'

It was too early, way too soon to tell her what he had feared when he had thought it was his fault that she wasn't pregnant. She had said that she had come into this marriage for very different reasons, but she hadn't said what they were. She didn't need to. She had already admitted that she didn't love him. But if she still wanted him then maybe it would be enough. Maybe it wasn't much on which to build a future, but it was better than nothing.

'It's my turn now. I promised you that if you told me your dearest wish then I would tell you mine. And I intend to keep that promise.'

Peta found that she was holding her breath, unable to speak.

'If we're being honest with each other, Peta, then there's something I want you to know. Something that matters as much to me as your Christmas wish does to you.'

'Go—go on.'

Reaching out, Liam took her hands in both of his, folding his warm, strong fingers around her finer, slimmer ones.

'I want you to believe that you were never—what did you say?—a ''brood mare'' to me. When I asked you to marry me, I said that I wanted children, yes—and I know that was the only reason my grandfather wanted me to marry. But it wasn't the only reason for me.'

'It wasn't?'

She still couldn't breathe properly and her voice sounded high and tight, coming from a painfully constricted throat.

'What, then?'

'Oh, Peta, do you have to ask?'

In contrast to hers, Liam's voice had dropped a deep, sexy octave. It was the sort of voice that sent shivers down her spine, made her heart clench. It wove spells around her, whispered in her ear of promises and dreams and the chance of happy-ever-after just as every good fairy story should have at its ending. But although it enticed and entranced, she didn't know if she should trust it. Surely it couldn't be that easy?

'I wanted you more than any woman I had wanted in my life. I couldn't live without you. I still can't. I can't let you go Peta, you're mine...'

His lips met hers in the softest of kisses, a kiss that stole away her heart, blurred her mind, left her incapable of thought, able only to respond.

And she wanted to respond. Needed to.

She had had enough of wanting, of yearning, of needing. She hated the loneliness and the emptiness and the hunger. That kiss held a promise of something—maybe only of tonight, maybe of more. She didn't know and she didn't care.

She only knew that she had been given a second chance at happiness, a second chance at her dream. And so she went into Liam's arms without care or hesitation, only feeling that here, at last, she had come home.

And here, at last she could be happy.

And if it only lasted tonight—well, she would cope with tomorrow when it came.

Liam's lovemaking was as slow and warm and ardent as she could ever have dreamed it might be. He carried her upstairs to the big bed in the room next door to where baby Alice, tucked up safely in her brand-new cot, slept the peaceful dreamless sleep of the very young. And there he eased the clothes from Peta's trembling body, warming her exposed skin with kisses that covered every inch, awakening the aching need that made her legs weaken beneath her.

She hadn't known that it was possible to be this aroused and still retain consciousness. Hadn't been aware of the endless sensual possibilities that could be created between hands and lips, and skin and nerves. She hadn't even considered how fast her heart could beat, how hot her blood could become. But tonight she learned it all, and understood that there were no limits to the pleasures of love that Liam could show her.

And when he finally sheathed his powerful body in her aching flesh she wept aloud at the sheer wonder and joy of it. Arching close to him, pressing every inch of herself against his hard form, she clutched at his shoulders, fingers digging into the taut muscles of his shoulders. She heard him groan her name, heard her own uncontrolled cry. And then she lost contact with the world in a shower of gold and silver stars and the heat and power of ecstasy.

Satiated and drained, worn out with delight, she couldn't move for a long, long time, and when she finally stirred it was only to curl herself up closer to the heat and comfort of Liam's relaxed, sprawling body. Already sleep was rolling over her in thick, heavy waves, and it was as she was drifting more than halfway out of consciousness that downstairs in the hall she heard the deep, sonorous tones of the grandfather clock striking the hour of twelve.

'Midnight,' Liam murmured lazily. 'It's Christmas Day. Happy Christmas, sweetheart.'

## CHAPTER THIRTEEN

CHRISTMAS DAY dawned bright and clear and crisp and cold. It was only as she stirred and stretched a lazy, dreamy hand out to where Liam had been lying the night before that Peta realised that part of the chill that affected her body was because the spot beside her where her husband should be lying was empty. And, to judge by the icy temperature of the sheets, if had been that way for quite some time.

Sitting up hastily in sudden surprise, she vaguely recalled a moment, obscenely early in the morning, when she had heard the shrill of the telephone, and Liam's groan as he had struggled awake enough to answer it.

His drowsiness had obviously not lasted, because she could remember the way his sleepy voice had sharpened, the way he had snapped a question into the receiver.

'Lucy! Darling, you don't know how good it is to hear from you! Where have you been? More important, where are you now?'

She had tried to stay awake, Peta remembered. She had wanted to hear the rest of the conversation. But exhausted sleep had overwhelmed her and Liam's voice had faded from her hearing before he had finished the phone call.

So where had he gone? Who *was* Lucy—other than Alice's mother, of course? And why had he been so delighted to hear from her?

She didn't have long to wonder because even as she stirred the sound of Alice whimpering in the next room brought her wide awake in a rush. The practicalities involved in getting the baby fed and clean and dressed occupied her fully for some time, and it was only when the tasks were finished that she had time to think of herself.

Sure that Liam must be home at any moment, she rushed through a shower and washed her hair, leaving it to dry loose and waving around her shoulders as she dressed in a deep-red chenille sweater and black velvet skirt. Downstairs in the sitting room the tree stood waiting, the brightly wrapped parcels lying around its base. Peta switched on the lights and sat down to watch them twinkle on and off, waiting impatiently.

Where *was* Liam? It was now almost midday and still there was no sign of him. After last night she had been so sure that they would share Christmas morning together, waking late and opening…

'Oh, the stocking! How could I forget?'

The recollection sent her flying up the stairs again, heading for the dressing room. She couldn't help smiling as she lifted the lid on the wicker laundry basket, thinking of how she hadn't been able to resist making up the Christmas stocking for Liam. She had bought lots of little presents, wrapping them all individually and stuffing them into the decorated velvet shape. She had come up with the perfect spot to hide it too, right at the bottom, underneath all the washing, carefully protected by a plastic bag. Liam would never have thought of looking in there.

It was as she pulled the stocking out that an unexpected sound caught her ears, making her pause. The rustle of paper didn't belong in amongst the washing.

It was the work of a moment to find the cause. The denim jeans that Liam had had pulled on in a temper on the morning after the party were almost at the bottom of the basket. And folded up many times, then pushed carelessly into a pocket, was a single sheet of paper.

A letter, Peta realised, opening it up and smoothing out the folds. A letter written in a hasty and barely legible scrawl. But it was the name at the bottom that caught and held her interest.

*Lucy.*

'Lucy! Darling, you don't know how good it is to hear from you!'

Liam's voice sounded so clearly in her thoughts that she actually swung round to see if he had come into the room.

*Lucy.* Who *was* Lucy?

And then her eye was caught by another name lower down the page.

Alice. *Her name is Alice.*

Lucy was Alice's mother. She knew that. But there was more to it than that.

Shaking her head to clear her thoughts, Peta forced herself to focus blurred eyes once more on the letter she held.

*Darling Liam…nowhere else to turn. But I know you'll look after her…I'll feel so much happier, knowing she's with you. That she's with family. Her name is Alice. Alice Tara Farrell.*

With *family. Alice Tara Farrell.*

The pain was terrible, tearing at her soul. She had never felt anything like it.

Alice Tara Farrell.

And Peta was back in the days, just over a year ago, before her wedding, when she and Liam had filled in forms and signed documents in order to obtain a marriage licence. And she had laughed at Liam's middle name.

'Liam Tara Farrell! But that's a girl's name—Tara!'

But Liam had brought his dark brows together in a furious frown and turned an appalling glare on her smiling face. He hadn't been at all amused. In fact he had been very angry indeed. And he had told her, in no uncertain terms, that Tara was not a girl's name at all. That it had been a royal name, the name of the long-ago High Kings of Ireland. And that it was also a name that was handed down through every member of his family.

*Every member of his family.*

Even Alice.

Too late, she looked back, seeing pictures in her mind. Pictures of Liam with Alice. His gentleness and concern for the tiny baby. His refusal to let Social Services in on the care of the little girl. His determination that she should have only the very best.

And worst of all she heard his voice saying 'Alice is my—' and hastily breaking off.

Alice is my…? There was only one word that fitted in that revealing space. That hastily covered mistake.

Alice is *my daughter.*

In the drive outside, the sound of a car crunching to a halt in the snow brought Peta's head up so fast that the tears she wasn't even aware of having shed spun off her cheeks and spattered onto the letter she still held.

Liam was back. And just at the moment when she really couldn't bear to see him.

But when she thought that she had hit the lowest point that it was possible to reach, she found that fate had one more blow in store for her.

It was as she came to the top of the stairs, standing and looking down to see the big front door open and Liam came inside, clearing the snow from his boots, that the big grandfather clock in the hallway started to strike the hour. And automatically Peta counted.

One…two…three…

She never got to the end. She didn't need to. Because it struck home like a flash of lightning just what time it was. It was noon. Twelve o'clock. And the memory of the same clock striking the same hour—but at midnight, not midday—brought with it a terrible, devastating memory that totally shattered her self-control.

'If you like, I'll have a little wager with you...' Liam had said. 'I'll bet that before midnight strikes to turn the Eve into Christmas Day itself you'll come to me and beg me to take you. And I'll be only too happy to do exactly as you want... We'll call it my Christmas present, shall we?'

'You bastard!'

Her cry of anger and shock echoed round the great hallway, barely dying away before Peta was stumbling down the stairs, launching herself from the next to bottom step and flinging herself at Liam, fists upraised to pound furiously and blindly at his broad shoulders.

'You rat! You pig! You selfish, unfeeling monster! I hate you! I hate you!'

'What the—?'

Taken totally by surprise, Liam took a hasty step backwards, his hands coming up in front of him to grab and capture her flailing fists and force them down, holding her prisoner.

'Peta, what's got into you? What's wrong?'

'What's wrong? What's *wrong?*'

She couldn't believe that he could be so calm, so completely in control. Did he have no conscience at all? Obviously not. And he must have known that at some point this would happen. Or had he really thought that he could get away with using her sexually, getting her to care for his child without her ever realising that she was being used in that way too?

'You know what's wrong—you...'

Her voice died on her as she heard a movement behind

Liam. The sound of another pair of footsteps, but lighter and softer than his.

'Liam?' a feminine voice asked uncertainly. 'What's going on? Who is this? And what is she in such a state about?'

'This…' Liam said, and to Peta's shock and horror there was actually a faint note of slightly shaken laughter in his voice. 'This is Peta—my darling wife. And I suspect that she's in such a state because she's found out about us.'

'I…' Peta tried to speak but could get no further. The words wouldn't form. Her head was awash with pain and bewilderment and despair. And she couldn't believe what she was seeing.

The owner of the second voice was a small, thin woman, no more than a girl, barely twenty if she was a day. She had long red hair, falling wildly around a narrow pale face, and her eyes were the brightest, most brilliant green that Peta had ever seen.

'Sweetheart…' Liam had turned back to her, but his use of that once affectionate word set a light to the blue touch-paper inside her head once more.

'Don't you *sweetheart* me! Don't you dare! You lying, cheating, brute, you—you—'

She couldn't think of anything bad enough to call him so instead she resorted to flinging a furious accusation into his deceitful face.

'I presume this—person—is Lucy—*"darling Lucy"?* Well, in that case, yes, I do know all about you! And about Alice—about your baby—Alice *Tara* Farrell. Your baby—and obviously Liam's daughter too!'

Her tirade fell into a stunned silence. A silence in which both Liam and Lucy stared at her in obvious amazement. And at the look on both their faces Peta felt both her certainty and the liberating anger start to recede.

Had she made a mistake? Was it possible? But how could she be wrong about this?

'Liam's daughter?' Lucy said shakily. 'How could Alice be Liam's daughter?'

Liam was watching Peta's face, his deep green eyes sharp as lasers, alert to every change in her mood so that he saw the sudden rush of doubt, the way that her confidence ebbed like a receding wave.

'Lucy, will you please tell Peta exactly who you are?'

Lucy glanced at Liam in obvious confusion, but then she turned to Peta and looked her straight in the eye.

'Liam is my brother. Well, my half-brother, really. We have the same father. So obviously Alice can't be Liam's. But he is her uncle.'

*Half-brother. We share the same father.* William Tara Farrell.

'My father spread his favours about a bit.'

Through the roaring in her head Peta heard Lucy turn to Liam.

'Where's Alice? Where's my baby.'

'She's upstairs.' He answered his sister but he kept his eyes on his wife's face. 'Upstairs. The first door on the left. She must be just waking around now.'

As Lucy ran up the stairs in search of the baby, Liam turned to Peta.

'It mattered that much to you?' he said unevenly. 'You cared that much? Peta…?'

But at last Peta had managed to find her voice.

'Liam—I'm sorry—I never thought…'

'I know. And I never thought to tell you. It was Lucy's secret, and I didn't think it was right to tell it until I'd found her and given her the chance to come back for Alice. She'd got involved with a man who wanted nothing to do with her once the baby was born and she was at the end of her tether. No money, no job. No prospect of things improving. Plus she was too stubborn to ask for help. Leaving Alice here with me was the only thing she could think to do.'

'I—I thought she was…'

'I know you did. But she isn't. I swear to you that that's the truth. If I already had a daughter then do you think that I'd have worried that I was—?'

The look on his face when he caught himself up told Peta that this was something she should know.

'That you were what?'

For a second she thought that he wasn't going to answer her, but then he looked her straight in the eyes, intent green gaze locking with confusion-clouded blue.

'I thought I was sterile when you didn't get pregnant.'

'You thought…? Oh, Liam! Did I do that to you? Darling, I'm so sorry—I would never have taken the Pill if I'd known it would make you think that way. And I never meant any of the terrible things I said. I just—'

'Peta, please!'

Peta froze, her words dying away as she registered what Liam had said. *Had* he said it? Had this husband of hers— the man who found it so very hard to say please—had he said just that—and to her? Her heart danced at just the thought of it.

And then he said it again.

'Peta, sweetheart, please will you stop talking and come here so that I can hold you?'

As he spoke he held out his arms to her, opening them wide so that there could be no doubt as to what he meant.

'*Please.* Please, my darling, I feel as if I'll die if I don't kiss you and tell you that I love you…'

And of course then there was nothing she could do but exactly what he asked.

Still dazed by what he had said, she moved forward as if in a dream and crushed herself tight up against the hard wall of his chest, her arms going round his waist and holding tightly. And as Liam's arms enfolded her, enclosing her in his strength and warmth, and his mouth came down on hers in a kiss of the purest, deepest love, it felt like really coming home.

'Peta, my love,' he said against her hair, 'I know I've made a terrible mess of things, but I want to put them right. If I made you think that I only married you because I wanted a child, then I couldn't have been more wrong. I wanted you and only you. I wanted you for yourself and because my life would be empty without you.'

'And mine without you,' Peta whispered, and was rewarded with another hug, a loving kiss pressed to her forehead.

'I didn't recognise what I felt as love because—well, to be honest, neither of my parents nor my grandfather were really great examples in that respect. I never expected it to be so huge—so overwhelming. It rocked my balance and I wasn't thinking straight for a while.'

'L-love does that,' Peta managed through tears of joy. 'It had much the same effect on me.'

'Please can we start again?'

*Please*, again. It seemed that once Liam had started to say the word he couldn't stop.

And suddenly, to her bewilderment, she found that her husband had released her and was down on one knee before her on the black and white tiled floor.

'I know this is a year late, that I should have done it the first time, but I hope you'll believe that this time it comes from the heart. Please can we start again? Can we make this marriage work—make it a real one—a true one—a marriage of love for the rest of our lives?'

Peta reached out for him, drew him to his feet and pressed a lingering kiss on his mouth.

'I can't think of anything I'd want more,' she said,

when at last she could speak. 'If I have you, and your love, then what else in the world could I need? This Christmas is going to be the best of my life.'

She had truly believed that she couldn't be happier. But it was only the following year that she learned what perfect happiness meant. When Liam put their newborn son into her arms just as Christmas Day dawned she knew then that her joy was truly complete.

**Modern Romance**™
...seduction and
passion guaranteed

**Tender Romance**™
...love affairs that
last a lifetime

**Sensual Romance**™
...sassy, sexy and
seductive

*Blaze*
...sultry days and
steamy nights

**Medical Romance**™
...medical drama on
the pulse

**Historical Romance**™
...rich, vivid and
passionate

*27 new titles every month.*

*With all kinds of Romance for
every kind of mood...*

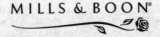

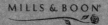

# FREE
## 2 BOOKS
### AND A SURPRISE GIFT!

We would like to take this opportunity to thank you for reading this Mills & Boon® book by offering you the chance to take TWO more specially selected titles from the Modern Romance™ series absolutely FREE! We're also making this offer to introduce you to the benefits of the Reader Service™—

★ FREE home delivery
★ FREE monthly Newsletter
★ FREE gifts and competitions
★ Exclusive Reader Service discount
★ Books available before they're in the shops

Accepting these FREE books and gift places you under no obligation to buy; you may cancel at any time, even after receiving your free shipment. Simply complete your details below and return the entire page to the address below. **You don't even need a stamp!**

**YES!** Please send me 2 free Modern Romance™ books and a surprise gift. I understand that unless you hear from me, I will receive 4 superb new titles every month for just £2.55 each, postage and packing free. I am under no obligation to purchase any books and may cancel my subscription at any time. The free books and gift will be mine to keep in any case.

P2ZEC

Ms/Mrs/Miss/Mr .......................................................Initials ...........................................
BLOCK CAPITALS PLEASE

Surname ...........................................................................................................................

Address ............................................................................................................................

..........................................................................................................................................

..........................................................................Postcode ...........................................

**Send this whole page to:**
**UK: FREEPOST CN81, Croydon, CR9 3WZ**
**EIRE: PO Box 4546, Kilcock, County Kildare (stamp required)**